There's No Escape

The sky looked as if it were on fire over to the west as the blazing red ball of the sun got ready to hit the water. *Sienna should be here to witness this,* Jason thought. It was one of the best sunsets he'd seen since he'd moved to Malibu.

He pulled out his cell to text Sienna. Before he'd gotten two letters in, he heard a creaking sound above him.

Jason froze.

Rotten wood creaks, he told himself. But he kept his body motionless, waiting for another sound.

Creak!

Footsteps? Jason wondered. *Sienna?* But they'd agreed to meet under the pier, not on it.

Jason slowly stretched out on his back. He stared up at the warped planks that made up the pier. Shafts of light filtered through each space between the planks. But with the next creak, some of that light was blocked.

The creaks were definitely footsteps. Somebody was up on the pier. And it wasn't Sienna.

Jason felt his heart start to race. He'd been on the beach when Tamburo shot him with a crossbow bolt. On the beach, alone, at sunset. Just like now. And Adam thought there might be more hunters around. Was a vampire hunter up on the old pier now, looking for him? Or, worse, *looking for Sienna?*

Sink your teeth into

Vampire BEACH

LEGACY

ALEX DUVAL

Simon Pulse
New York • London • Toronto • Sydney

To Peter Sharoff

SIMON PULSE
An imprint of Simon & Schuster Children's Publishing Division
1230 Avenue of the Americas, New York, NY 10020
Copyright © 2007 by Working Partners Limited
All rights reserved, including the right of reproduction in whole or in part in any form.
SIMON PULSE and colophon are registered trademarks of Simon & Schuster, Inc.
Designed by Steve Kennedy
The text of this book was set in Adobe Caslon.
Manufactured in the United States of America
First Simon Pulse edition June 2007
10 9 8 7 6 5 4 3
Library of Congress Control Number 2006937103
ISBN-13: 978-1-4169-1169-2
ISBN-10: 1-4169-1169-3

Special thanks to Laura Burns and Melinda Metz

Vampire BEACH

LEGACY

ONE

"There's this juicy French girl I'm trying to seduce," Jason Freeman told his juicy French girlfriend, Sienna Devereux. "I need to have some lines ready to go."

"I'm almost positive Madame Goddard isn't going to have pickup lines on the test." Sienna laughed. She pointed to the French textbook lying open between them on her bed. "I am *also* almost positive that some version of this reading comprehension exercise *will* be. So read this story about Jacques and Pauline at the Tour de France aloud, and then I'll ask you questions."

"Who cares about Jacques and Pauline?" Jason replied. "All I can think about is the French babe."

"Oh, yeah?" Sienna raised one eyebrow. "What's this girl like?"

Jason opened his mouth to answer.

"In French," Sienna added.

"*Très jolie. Et*, um, *très* . . ." Jason struggled to come up with more French words for a moment, then gave it up. "She's way gorgeous. Long black hair. These killer lips. Amazing legs." He slid one arm around Sienna's waist.

He could hardly believe that he and Sienna were

officially together now. And, thankfully, Brad Moreau—Sienna's old boyfriend, and one of Jason's first buddies when he started DeVere High at the beginning of senior year—was actually okay with the whole deal.

"This girl clearly has a lot of depth," Sienna teased, playfully slapping Jason's arm away.

"Oh, I'm just getting started," Jason said quickly. "She's insanely smart. She always knows where the best parties are. And you know what else?"

"What?" Sienna asked, her dark eyes warm as she looked at him.

"She's a vampire, which means she has super-strength. You should see her play beach volleyball."

"Hmmm. And you think you have enough to offer this fabulous French vampire goddess woman? You, a mere mortal?" Sienna asked.

"Well, in the sixth grade I won a hot-dog-eating contest," Jason answered. Sienna snickered. "Plus, when a car breaks down, I can dial AAA with incredible speed. No one's faster. I have also been told—admittedly by my little sister—that I am the less British version of Jude Law. What more could any French vampire goddess woman want?"

Sienna burst into giggles. It was good to see her laugh. Sienna hadn't done much laughing since the crossbow killer started murdering vampires in Malibu right before Christmas. The guy—who had turned out to be a detective with the Malibu PD—had mistaken Jason for a vampire and shot him on the first night of the hunt. If the crossbow bolt had landed an inch or two lower, Jason would be dead.

Dominic Ames, a vampire and longtime boyfriend of Belle Rémy, Sienna's best friend, *was* dead. So was a human girl Detective Tamburo had wrongly assumed was a vampire. Tamburo had planned to kill Sienna on the last night of his vampire-hunting cycle. He'd actually had her in his car while Jason had been right behind in his VW Beetle, trying to get to Sienna before it was too late. An 18-wheeler had been caught up in the middle of their car chase, and Tamburo's El Dorado had shot off one of the cliffs in the Malibu hills. He died. Sienna lived—but only thanks to a transfusion of Jason's blood, straight from his wrist.

"Of course, I can also burp the Pledge of Allegiance," Jason went on. He knew he was being a dumbass, but he just wanted to keep Sienna laughing a little longer. It was the beginning of February, and she still wasn't quite back to her usual self. She was a little quieter. A little more serious. A little less . . . Sienna.

Jason could tell that it was mostly because Belle was so messed up. She was grieving for Dominic in a huge way. Sienna had been going to therapy sessions with Belle because Belle found it impossible to do them by herself, and Sienna's parents had insisted Sienna get some therapy of her own, too. They thought she needed help dealing with the trauma of almost being a victim of the crossbow killer.

"Enough goofing around. Back to the book," Sienna instructed. "You have to pass French or you don't graduate. And I'm telling you one thing right now: There's no way I'm going out with a high school boy once I'm in college." She gave him a teasing smile.

"This French thing is unjust," Jason said. "I already have foreign language credits. I took two years of Spanish back in Michigan."

"In case you haven't noticed, this isn't Michigan," Sienna replied. "That sound you hear? That whooshing? We call that the o-cean. That's one way you can tell you're not in Michigan."

"O-cean," Jason repeated slowly.

"Or, *en Français, la mer*," Sienna added. "*Répètes, s'il te plait.*"

"*La mer.*"

"*Donne-moi un baiser chaud et mouillé, bébé,*" Sienna said, in flawless French. "*Répètes, s'il te plait.*"

"*Donne-moi un baiser chaud et mou-something, bébé,*" Jason said, attempting to *répètes* what Sienna had just said.

Sienna gave him a slow smile, then leaned over and kissed him.

"What was that for?" Jason asked. "Not that I'm complaining."

"You wanted a line to snag your French girl, so I gave you one. You just said, 'Give me a hot, wet kiss, baby,'" Sienna explained.

"I did?" Jason tried to remember the words he'd mangled. "Well, I always did have a way with the ladies. How do I say it again?"

"*Donne-moi un baiser chaud et mouillé, bébé,*" Sienna told him.

"All right, all right, I'll kiss you. You don't have to beg," Jason teased. He threw the French textbook to the floor, pressed Sienna back against the pillows, and kissed her.

Sienna pushed him away before he'd had nearly enough of her. "Not in front of the children!" she teased, gesturing to the mound of stuffed animals that had come with the parade of get well cards after her "car accident."

Jason's blood had helped Sienna heal from her severe wounds almost instantly. But the vampires of DeVere Heights were very careful about keeping up the appearance of being human, which meant that after a near-fatal car crash, Sienna would have weeks of "recovery," accompanied by weeks of visits by friends with cards and presents, most of the presents being stuffed animals.

"The children like to see Mommy and Daddy getting along," Jason joked, and kissed her again.

"You need to study," Sienna said at last. "I told you, if you don't graduate, I'm going to have to find myself a new guy."

Jason leaned off the bed and picked up the French book. "Fine. But there are a lot of good-looking high school girls. I might just find myself somebody new too."

"Yeah, right." Sienna took the book and flipped back to the page they'd been working on. "Jacques and Pauline at the Tour de France..."

They kept at it for an hour. French, French, more French, nothing but French. "*La classe est terminée,*" Sienna finally said, closing the book. "Class dismissed."

Jason let himself flop back on the bed. He loved hanging out in Sienna's room. He wouldn't want it for his own, but there was something about spending a little time in her space—all candles and sheer curtains around the bed, and more pillows than any human could ever use—that just made him feel good.

"I'm kicking you out now," Sienna told him cheerfully. "My mom and I always watch *Project Runway* together, and it's about to start. She'll be miffed if I miss it. Besides, it's kind of fun."

"You vampires and your rituals," Jason mock-complained as he stood up.

It had been an adjustment getting together with a vampire. A big adjustment. For one thing, it meant accepting that Sienna had to feed on other guys. That had felt like a punch in the gut the first few times it had happened, even though she made sure to do it in private, not right in the middle of the dance floor at a party or something, the way a lot of vampires did.

He'd come to terms with that one—basically because he'd *had* to, but there were still times when he felt like a complete outsider. There were a lot of secrets about the way vampire society operated that Sienna wasn't free to tell him. In spite of it all, though, being with a vampire had started to feel surprisingly ordinary.

Sienna walked Jason over to the door and kissed him, her arms wrapped around his neck. "You know what? I want to tell you something," she said when the kiss ended. Her lips were still just a breath away from his.

"What?" Jason asked. She suddenly sounded so serious.

"I just feel . . . safe when you're around. Safe and happy. My parents should be paying you instead of that therapist I see," Sienna told him, her dark eyes intense. "You have made my life a better place to be."

Jason smiled. "So, how much money are we talking here?" he began. "What kind of bucks does your therapist . . ." He let the sentence trail off. What she'd said was too big to joke about. The fact that she trusted him in that way meant everything to him. "I'm always going to be here for you, whenever you need me," he said seriously. "I promise."

TWO

My life just can't get any better, Jason thought.

He couldn't stop smiling as he steered the Bug home. He knew he was being kind of a geek, but what Sienna had said had made his night. That and the fact that she'd been willing to spend hours helping him with his French.

Most of their friends were at the beach, the movies, or the mall, indulging in full-on cases of Senioritis. Their college apps were in. The schools had their transcripts and their SAT scores and their recommendations—everything the admissions officers would use to make their decisions. What Jason and the other seniors did this last semester didn't really matter. Unless they really screwed up, by, say, not passing French, which was a required subject at DeVere High for some insane reason—probably because the money for the DeVere Library and the DeVere Symphony Space and the DeVere Athletic Complex and almost everything else that was cultural in Malibu was funded by the Devereux family, who happened to be French. Just like almost every important family in Malibu.

And all those French-ancestored, very important families, also happened to be vampiric and living in DeVere Heights. Where else? Jason suspected that he and his family were practically the only regular humans who lived in Malibu's most exclusive gated community. And he *knew* he was one of the very few regular humans who'd made it into the über-popular group at DeVere High.

Sienna could have been out having fun with any of those übers tonight, Jason thought as he pulled into his driveway. He knew she could have been indulging in some Senioritis of her own. Instead, she'd chosen to help her French-challenged boyfriend study. He grinned. He was one lucky individual.

As he climbed out of the car he heard the soft purr of his friend Adam Turnball's Vespa pulling in behind him. Turnball—as in, not of French ancestry, not even especially good in French! Adam was mid-level popular at DeVere High, except to the movie nerds— Adam was a god to them—and definitely not a vampire.

"What's up, my brother?" Adam called as he parked the moped. "Is everything copacetic?"

Jason laughed. Who but Adam talked like that? "Ultra copacetic," he answered. "Come on in. Mom hit Malibu Kitchen today. Let's see what she brought home." He led the way into the house and straight to

the kitchen. His father sat at the table, brow furrowed, shoulders hunched, surrounded by stacks of
papers, forms, and receipts. A calculator was posi-
tioned at his elbow.

"Hey, Dad, we're doing a food raid," Jason
announced.

"I always fast before I come over," Adam told Mr.
Freeman. "I like to have belly room because you guys
always have the best chow."

Mr. Freeman answered with a grunt. *Weird!* Jason
thought. *He usually talks too much to my friends.*

"What are you in the mood for?" Jason asked
Adam, opening the closest cupboard. It was only then
that his brain registered what his eyes had just seen:
forms, receipts, calculator, cranky and distracted
father. Jason knew these could mean only one thing:
His dad was in the middle of his usual February pre-
tax family financial review. A financial review that
would include Jason's college fund, which happened
to be seven thousand dollars light for a reason that
Jason absolutely could not explain to his parents. He'd
withdrawn the cash to buy back a vampire artifact that
his friend Tyler had stolen and pawned. That was the
kind of thing parents just didn't understand.

All the saliva in Jason's mouth dried up. His father
was going to go ballistic. *Maybe I'm wrong,* Jason told
himself. *I could be wrong.* He swallowed hard, then

forced out the words, "Whatcha workin' on, Dad?" while peering over at the table to see if statements for his college fund account were in the mess of papers.

"Just going over our financial stuff so I won't go nuts at tax time," his father answered.

Adam's eyes widened. Jason could see he understood that they had walked into a Code Red situation here.

"Hey, you know what? There's a *Godfather* marathon on tonight. It's starting . . . basically now," Adam said. "We all have to watch it. We're men. That's what we do. We watch *The Godfather*, then quote it on all occasions to the bafflement of womankind," he finished in a rush.

"Yeah, Dad. You've got ages to worry about taxes," Jason added, getting on board with Adam's Plan of Distraction. "Let's do *The Godfather*. I'll get snacks."

"'Leave the gun, take the cannoli,'" Adam encouraged, already quoting. "Now that has to be an offer you can't refuse, Mr. Freeman," he added in his best Brando imitation.

Jason's father twisted his neck from side to side, trying to work out the kinks. "I'm almost done here, and it's wiped me out. I'll have to take a pass."

Almost done? Jason thought. Surely that meant that at any minute his dad was going to find out about the missing cash.

"I completely forgot. I didn't do my chem homework for tomorrow. I should take off," Adam said, inching toward the door.

Rat attempting to abandon sinking ship, Jason thought. Well, there was no way he was letting this rat leave. As long as Adam stayed, the extreme badness that was about to rain down on Jason would be delayed. And the delay would give Jason's dad some cool-down time.

"You can use my chem book," Jason told Adam, giving his friend a meaningful glare. "I need to finish up the assignment, anyway."

Adam replied with a reluctant okay-okay-I'll-stay nod, and Jason turned back to the cupboard. "Here, we'll take these wasabi peas," he said, hurling the bag at his friend. "And, um, this black licorice." He tossed the package over his shoulder in Adam's direction and heard it hit the ground. "And now a couple of sodas." He plucked two Dr Peppers out of the fridge. "So let's get upstairs to the Wonderful World of Chemistry." Jason started out of the kitchen, knowing Adam would follow.

"Jason," his father called.

Jason stopped. This was it. His life was over.

He turned around.

"Don't blow up the house," Mr. Freeman joked.

"Just pens and paper, no chemicals," Jason answered,

wondering if his father could possibly have forgotten to look at his account.

Mr. Freeman stood up and started gathering his piles of receipts together. "I think we're in decent shape for April. The—" He was interrupted by his cell. He pulled it out of his pocket and checked the screen. "It's work. I'll take it upstairs. I might need the computer," he said.

Jason felt like the oxygen in the room had turned to helium. That's how relieved he was. As soon as his dad left, Jason rushed over to the table.

"Do you think he could have forgotten how much money you were supposed to have in the account?" Adam asked as Jason scanned the piles of paper for his college account statements.

"By a few hundred bucks, yeah. By several thousand, no way," Jason replied, spotting the statements and snatching them up. The most recent one was on top. And the total . . . was exactly what his father would have been expecting. *Not* minus seven thousand. Jason stared at it, his mind whirling. The account was exactly as it had been pre-pawn shop. The seven thousand dollars had miraculously reappeared.

His dad must have checked only the current total, because down a few statements it was clear that Jason had taken out the cash—right when Tyler had rolled into town from Michigan. Tyler had owed his drug dealer some serious cash, so when he had gone to a party at Zach Lafrenière's place—Lafrenière, as in French ancestry, as in vampire—he hadn't been able to resist picking up a silver chalice that looked like it was worth enough to save his butt.

It was. But the chalice was also an heirloom used in sacred vampire rituals, and the vampires were not at all happy that it was gone. In fact, they had planned to kill Tyler in retribution. Jason had managed to save his friend's life. And then he'd bought back the chalice in a gesture of goodwill. In the end, the only thing that had got hurt was his college fund.

"Somebody put the money back," Jason told Adam. "There's a statement—a statement I'm going to, um, disappear," he added, folding the statement and putting it in his pocket, "that shows me taking seven thousand out. Then, three weeks later, it shows that there was a deposit for seven thousand going back in."

"Hmm. Looks like you were the recipient of a special grant," Adam said. He tore open the bag of wasabi peas he still held and popped a handful in his mouth. "Dr Pepper! Now!" He stuck out his tongue and fanned it with his free hand.

Jason handed him a soda, and Adam drank it down. "I love those things, but I always forget how insanely hot they are," he explained.

"You're not supposed to scarf them." Jason laughed.

Adam coughed a couple of times, then cleared his throat. "As I was saying, it seems like someone made a contribution to the Jason Freeman Needy Boy Foundation."

"Who would do something like that?" Jason asked. "Not that I don't appreciate it, but I can't think of anyone who—"

A car horn cut him off.

"That's for me!" Jason's sister Danielle called from upstairs. "Wave or blink the lights or something to let them know I'm coming."

"Remember when Dani didn't think she'd have any friends at her new school?" Adam asked.

"Yeah, for that whole day and a half," Jason replied as they walked over to the front door. He flipped the porch light on and off.

"Who's out there, anyway?" Adam said, peering through the long, narrow window next to the door.

"Kristy, of course," Jason said, taking a look. "She and Dani start to wither if they are apart for more than eight hours. And that's Maria, Billy . . . and I think Ryan Patrick from down the block is driving." Jason turned to Adam. "So what's our thinking on Ryan? He spent last semester in Paris as an exchange student. He lives in DeVere Heights. But Patrick is not a French last name."

"True. But he's always been a member of the V-crowd, ever since we were kids," Adam answered. "I think odds are that he's a Friend of Dracula."

"Where are you off to?" Jason asked as Dani rushed toward the door. The heels of her leopard-print Stella McCartney shoes—the ones she "love, love, *loved* and could not live without"—were clicking on the tile of the entryway, and her auburn hair was flying around her face.

"Big date?" Adam chimed in.

"No, just the movies. No parties on Wednesday night. Nothing juicy," Dani explained.

"Just the movies," Adam repeated, shaking his head sadly as Dani hurried out to the car. "Even a bad movie is better than pretty much anything else the world has to offer."

"You need to get out more," Jason told Adam as he watched his sister and her friends drive off. He didn't think he'd ever seen Ryan in the mix before. But at this point, Dani had even more friends in Malibu than she'd had in Michigan. And that was saying something. He could only really keep track of the key players.

"So you want to hang by the pool for a while?" Jason asked his friend. "Oh wait. No, you have all that chemistry homework to get to."

"Smart-ass," Adam answered. He headed back through the kitchen and straight out the French doors to the pool. "Although I really do have homework. I've been spending too much time on my extracurricular project."

"Still?" Jason asked.

"Still!" Adam repeated, sitting down on the diving board. "Excuse me for wanting to make sure another vampire hunter doesn't slide into town. I want us to be prepared next time."

"Tamburo *was* the first one since the Renaissance," Jason pointed out. Like he'd pointed out several times before.

"That doesn't mean it will be centuries until another one shows," Adam argued, as he always did. "The bad thing is, I'm having a hard time finding any solid info on the web. It's all Van Helsing and Buffy and Blade and the Belmont clan."

"The who?" Jason asked.

"It's from this Japanese video game series, *Castlevania*," Adam told him. "It's fun, but not useful. I—"

The French doors swung open. "Guys, what, no *Godfather* marathon?" Mr. Freeman called. "I got my second wind. And I made popcorn!"

Adam turned his head to hide his laughter.

"We're there," Jason called back. He glanced at his friend. "It was your idea. Looks like you're stuck watching a Mafia-fest."

"Oh, like I'm going to complain about that," Adam said, getting up. "You really dodged a bullet tonight, you know."

"I know." Jason grinned, still feeling a little heli-umed out. "I've got good friends, a truly amazing girl-friend, Dani is happy, the parents are happy, there's an actual swimming pool in the backyard, and since my dad is ignorant of the seven grand I spent on non-college-related expenses, I can live to enjoy it all!"

"And we're about to watch *The Godfather*," Adam added as they headed inside.

"And that," Jason agreed. "Life is good."

THREE

The life-loving feeling was still there the next day at lunch, when Jason and Adam headed out to the huge balcony overlooking the ocean. Sometimes Jason still had trouble wrapping his head around the fact that this was part of his school cafeteria.

He spotted Sienna and Belle at one of the larger tables, and his pace automatically picked up. He slid onto the bench next to Sienna, put down his tray of food, and gave her a quick hello kind of kiss. As he started to pull away, Sienna wrapped her fingers in his hair and pulled him back, keeping the kiss going. "Not in front of the children," Jason finally said, jerking his chin toward Adam and Belle.

Sienna laughed. Jason couldn't get enough of that laugh!

"We have our own Romeo and Juliet at the table," Belle said to Adam.

"Are we talking the Baz Luhrmann or the Franco Zeffirelli variety?" Adam asked.

Belle looked helplessly at Jason. "Translation?"

"Can't help you," Jason told her. "I'm pretty sure he's slipped into film-speak."

"Okay, I'll forgive you for not knowing Zeffirelli," Adam said. "But Baz? He's one of the greatest directors of our time. *Moulin Rouge!* anyone?"

"Sorry," Belle answered, shaking her head.

"Wasn't there singing in it?" Jason asked. "I don't do movies with singing."

Adam turned to Sienna. "You're my last hope. Tell me you saw *Moulin Rouge!*"

"I think I was, like, twelve, when that came out," Sienna protested.

Adam leaned across the table toward her as if he were imparting a great secret. "There's this new invention. A machine that lets you play movies on your TV screen whenever you want to!" he told her. "The movies come on these cool little discs—they look like crêpes, but smaller, and thinner, and metallic. With this machine, you can watch movies that were made before you were even born!"

"Maybe I'll check it out sometime." Sienna laughed.

"Not with me," Jason teased.

Brad Moreau dropped his tray onto the table and sat down next to Jason. "What's the topic?" he asked. Ryan Patrick and Maggie Roy were with him.

"Please tell me one of you knows who Baz Luhrmann is," Adam pleaded.

"Can't help you," Brad said.

"Didn't he direct those Chanel commercials with Nicole Kidman?" Maggie asked.

"Yes!" Adam cried. "They show some of his trademark Italian operatic influences."

"Like in *Moulin Rouge*!" Ryan added.

"Thank God!" Adam exclaimed. "I thought I'd entered some unholy dimension where I would never be able to communicate with the natives."

"I'll watch anything that's set in Paris," Ryan said. "It's hands down my favorite city. I hated coming back after living there last semester—although it was almost worth leaving just for the going-away party. It was wild; we snuck down into the catacombs. I was having so much fun I lost track of time. Almost missed my flight."

Maggie ran her fingers through Ryan's curly blond hair. "Well, we're all glad to have you back."

"You're going to be extra glad, because I'm throwing a Valentine's Day party that will be extreme," Ryan continued. "It's a week from Friday, and you're all invited to come and make complete fools of yourselves."

"Too bad Zach's still going to be in Australia," Maggie commented.

"Yeah, it's so horrible that he has to be out of school, spending days on the beach, hanging out with all the actors in his mom's movie," Sienna joked.

"My party is going to be wilder than any movie set," Ryan said. He turned to Jason. "Think you can be there?"

Why is Ryan singling me out? Jason thought. *He hardly knows me.* But a Valentine's Day party—with his new Valentine, Sienna? He wasn't going to pass that up. "Absolutely," Jason told Ryan. "Thanks."

"Cool. Bring your sister. If she wants to invite some of her friends, that's cool too," Ryan said.

"Oh. Okay." Jason frowned as he took a swig of his Coke. He had the strangest feeling that Ryan was really just trying to make sure Dani would show.

Sienna pulled him out of his thoughts by leaning close and whispering into his ear. "There are no parties *this* weekend. But I have an idea," she breathed.

The bell rang. Jason stood up, grabbing his tray and Sienna's. "So what is it?" he asked as they walked back inside together.

"Gotta go," Sienna teased. "I'll have to tell you later. Just make sure you have Sunday free. All day."

Jason dumped their trash and stacked the trays on top of the garbage can as Sienna headed off to class. "A hint. I need a hint," he called after her.

"I'll be there," Sienna threw back over her shoulder. "Do you need to know more?"

Actually, he didn't.

It was Sunday morning, and Jason was driving toward the marina with Adam.

"I'm definitely not complaining about an invitation

to spend the day on a yacht," Adam said. "But wouldn't you and Sienna prefer to be alone?"

"Sienna likes to make sure Belle has plans every weekend since she's still so ripped up about Dominic. And she didn't have anything going for today," Jason answered. "Besides, it's not like the yacht is so small that we all have to be on top of each other. "

He pulled into one of the parking spots in the marina's lot. Sienna's Spider was parked a few cars away. "They beat us here."

"Well, I hope they waited for us," Adam joked. "Otherwise I'll have to go home and watch *Titanic* just to console myself."

Jason led the way over to the Devereux berth, slowing as they approached the gigantic boat anchored there. "*That's* the yacht?" he asked, disbelieving. "I mean, it's beautiful, but it looks more like a paper airplane than a yacht."

"I heard that," Sienna called from the top of the gangplank. "I'll have you know this is a WallyPower 118. There are only three of these in existence."

"Wait. This is the yacht from *The Island*? The *Renovatio*!" Adam exclaimed.

"Not this exact one. But one of them, yeah," Sienna told him as they walked up the gangplank toward her.

"Hardcore," Adam said approvingly. "This day is going to be even better than I thought!"

When they reached the top, Sienna took Jason's hand. "This is Lee Osbourne, our captain for the day," she announced, smiling at a tanned, thirty-something guy who'd appeared next to her. His dark hair was pulled back into a ponytail, and he wore an easy grin.

"Call me Oz," he said. "You guys ready for your first Wally ride?"

"Absolutely," Jason replied.

"Head on in to the lounge then, folks," Oz instructed. "Lunch will be served later. Until then, there are some drinks and snacks to hold you."

"Come on, guys," Sienna said. "Belle's already in there."

Sienna led the way into a vast combination lounge/dining area/cockpit. Jason stopped at the top of the stairs and took it all in. Windows wrapped around the whole enormous area, so it felt like you were outside, even though you were inside. The view was breathtaking.

Belle was already in full-on relaxation mode, clad in a tiny bikini and lying on her back on one of the cushy sofas. The diamond of her belly ring sparkled in the morning sunlight. "Do you think Captain Oz has some lemons on board?" she asked. "I want to squeeze some juice into my hair."

"I don't think Oz is in charge of lemons, but I'll

check with the chef," Sienna promised. "Be right back." She disappeared down the stairs.

"The *chef*? This is all a little too much for the child of the poor but humble sheriff," Adam joked. "How am I ever going to be content when you return me to my hovel, now that I've seen how the other half lives?" He stretched out on one of the sofas and gave a sigh of contentment.

Jason took a seat across from his friend. "We'll start a fund for you," he answered.

"I'll contribute," Belle volunteered.

"Really?" Adam asked. "Will you hock that sparkly you've got stuck in your belly button, because that'd go a long way toward—" He stumbled to a stop, and Jason could see why; Belle's eyes had filled with tears.

"Hey, are you okay?" Jason asked.

"Yeah. Sorry," Belle said, wiping away her tears. "It's just that Dominic gave me this." She pointed to her belly ring.

"I didn't . . . Sorry, I didn't mean to remind you of . . ." Adam's voice trailed off. He looked miserable.

"It's okay," Belle told him. "Really. It's not your fault. I think about him all the time, anyway."

She's so torn up, Jason thought. He tried to imagine how he'd feel if anything ever happened to Sienna. But his brain refused to go there.

"Lemons!" Sienna called as she ran back up the

stairs. "I scored a whole bag!" She hesitated on the top step. "What's up?" she asked, clearly sensing the change in mood.

"What's up is that we want our lemons," Jason answered, his voice coming out a little too loud and jolly, like somebody on a low-budget TV commercial.

"Jason decided he needs some highlights," Adam added. "He's going to juice his hair too."

Sienna laughed and tossed one of the lemon halves at Jason. "You should. I think you could use some streaks, don't you, Belle?" She dropped onto the couch next to her friend and put a CD in the player.

"Absolutely," Belle answered, managing a smile. She took one of the lemon halves and squeezed some juice onto her short blond hair, then used her fingers to comb it through.

"How about a game of 'I never' before lunch?" Sienna asked. "Belle rules at that game."

Jason and Adam exchanged a "huh?" look. "Never heard of it," Jason told her.

"I guess it's more of a slumber party thing," Sienna said. "We haven't played it in forever."

"Ooooh, I'm in," Adam said immediately. "I've always wanted to know what goes on at a slumber party."

"Okay, here's how it works. We all start out with, like, ten Tic Tacs each." Sienna pulled a plastic container of the mints from her bag and shook ten out into her palm, then handed the container to Belle. "Then we go around in the circle, and—you know what, it's easier just to start. I'll go first. I never ate an artichoke. Now, if you have eaten an artichoke, you have to give me one of your Tic Tacs," she announced.

"Wait," Adam said. "Are you telling me you've never eaten an artichoke?"

"They smell like feet," Sienna told him, wrinkling her nose. "But if you've eaten them, anyway, you owe me a mint. That's how it works."

"Bor-ing," Belle teased. Everyone gave Sienna a mint. "My turn," Belle said. She glanced from Sienna to Adam to Jason, an actual smile on her face now. "I never made out on a first date."

"You're not supposed to lie in this game, by the way," Sienna pointed out.

"I'm not lying!" Belle protested. "Although maybe it depends on how you define 'date.' Or 'making out.' By my definition, I haven't. Now give me a Tic Tac, wench."

Sienna flicked one of the little mints at Belle. Jason handed one over too. *We definitely made out on our first date,* he thought. *Hell, we made out when Sienna was still with Brad. But was she thinking of me when she gave Belle that Tic Tac, or somebody else?*

Adam sighed loudly and hung on to all of his mints.

Belle winked at him. "Now we know who the hos are," she joked. Then she turned to Jason. "You're up."

"I never went on *Jerry Springer* with my two girl-friends and my chimp," Jason said.

Jason didn't get any Tic Tacs, but everybody laughed, which was all he was going for. Sienna still needed to up her daily laugh quota. And Belle needed a quota, period.

By the time lunch—cajun chicken and a mesclun field greens salad with Champagne dressing—was served up, Adam was ahead by seven or eight mints.

"Time for you to go down," Jason warned his friend, forking a bite of salad into his mouth. "I never saw *Citizen Kane*."

Adam threw a Tic Tac into Jason's salad. Belle and Sienna didn't have to pay up. They hadn't seen it either.

"What's that movie even about?" Belle asked.

"It's about this man who is tortured by—" Adam began.

"No, don't even tell me," Belle begged. "I had to turn the DVD off in the middle of *Saw III*. The torture scenes were too gross."

"Not that kind of torture," Adam told her. "He was tortured by memories of his past, you know, the choices he'd made."

"Sounds kinda boring," Belle commented.

Jason glanced at Adam's head, looking for signs of imminent explosion.

"I never saw *Apocalypse Now*," Sienna challenged, before Adam could formulate a response to Belle.

Adam squeezed his eyes shut in pain, then handed over a Tic Tac. Jason and Belle didn't.

"I hate those movies about the end of the world. Everything looks so ugly. Especially the clothes. Who wants to watch that?" Belle asked. "Like the one with the people who were hiding out from zombies in a mall—*Dawn of the Dead*. I mean, they were in a mall, and they never bothered to change out of their grungy clothes! And did I say they were in a *mall*, as in *lots of stores*?"

"That actually isn't the kind of apocalypse in—" Adam stopped himself. "You know what? Never mind. It's your turn," he told Belle.

"I never saw . . ." Belle hesitated.

"*Heathers*," Jason stage-whispered.

"I never saw *Heathers!*" Belle exclaimed. "I really never did."

"Unfair. I'm being ganged up on," Adam complained, giving up another mint. "And I can't believe none of you have seen *Heathers*."

"What's it about?" Belle asked.

"This group of girls who torment the less popular—"

"So it's like *Mean Girls*," Belle interrupted. "Grool! You know—'I meant to say cool and then I started to say great'? I just love that!"

Adam groaned. "No comparison. *Heathers* isn't a piece of teen fluff. It's a revolutionary mix of teen comedy, black comedy, absurd comedy, and social commentary on popularity. Plus, there's lots of violence. And croquet."

"As usual, you've lost me," Jason told him.

"You know, I think my sister left a copy of that movie in the cabinet in the stateroom. Not that it ever gets watched—my father practically refuses to remove *The Godfather* from the DVD player," Sienna said.

"'Leave the gun . . . ,'" Adam began.

"'Take the cannoli,'" Jason finished for him.

Sienna and Belle looked at each other.

"Do you know what they're talking about?" Belle asked.

"No, and I don't care," Sienna answered, shooting a wink at Jason.

Adam shook his head. "I'm giving you that one, because it's not a girl thing. But *Heathers*? Everybody should see *Heathers*."

The chef appeared with plates of Snickers pie.

"I'll watch it with you," Belle volunteered. "We can take our dessert to the stateroom."

"Sounds fun," Sienna said.

"Not you," Belle told her. "You and Romeo stay up here and try to come up with something that's on my 'I never' list." She winked, then grabbed her pie and headed belowdecks. Adam grinned and followed.

"Those are some good friends," Jason commented.

"Very good friends," Sienna agreed. "I'm glad you got Adam to come. He makes Belle laugh. Not many people can do that lately."

"I'm glad he came, and I'm glad he's gone away for a little while," Jason answered.

"Me too." Sienna leaned across the table and kissed him. She tasted like the dessert. But better. Much, much better.

"Let's go out on deck." Sienna took him by the hand and led him out into the salty ocean air. The sound of Louis Armstrong singing "What a Wonderful World" blended with the waves.

"I love this song," Sienna said. "In fact, I'm decreeing this our official song."

"That's how it works? By decree of Sienna?" Jason asked.

"How else?" she replied. "It's now our song, and that means we must dance to it every time we hear it."

Jason wasn't complaining. He'd be happy to dance with Sienna any time, any place, to any music. He pulled her into his arms and began to sway to the rhythm, her body pressed against his.

Now this *is dancing*, Jason thought. The moment was absolutely perfect. Except for the part where his *good* friend Adam was loudly clearing his throat from ten feet away. Reluctantly, Jason pulled away from Sienna.

"Um, sorry to interrupt, but some guys on a speed-boat are taking pictures of us," Adam explained.

"They're serious about it too," Belle said from behind him, her voice tinged with panic. "They've got paparazzi-worthy zoom lenses."

"Where?" Jason asked.

"Right side," Adam answered.

Jason immediately started for the railing, Sienna on his heels.

"Why would they want pictures of us?" Belle asked as she and Adam followed. She sounded freaked. Way too freaked for what was actually happening. Jason figured that after Dominic's murder, Belle scared a lot more easily.

He put a reassuring hand on her arm. "I'm sure it's no big deal," he said, trying to sound casual. "They probably just saw you and Sienna and mistook you for Cameron Diaz and Angelina Jolie."

That got a little smile from Belle.

"I'm confused," Sienna said. "Is that them?"

Jason looked where she was pointing. All he saw was a couple of college-age guys in a speedboat, sucking down some beers. He shot a questioning look at Adam.

"That's them. But they got their camera stuff stowed pretty quickly," Adam commented. "Maybe they realized we caught them in the act."

"Ahoy, me beauties!" one of the guys, a redhead with a scruffy goatee, shouted to Belle and Sienna as his buddy powered the boat closer. "Care to board us?" Goatee and his bud laughed like that was the funniest thing they'd ever heard.

"You're drunk!" Sienna yelled back.

"Not too drunk to show you girls a good time," Goatee answered, getting more laughs from his friend.

"My analysis? Obnoxious, but not dangerous," Sienna said, turning her back on the speedboat. "But let's lose them anyway." She led the way to the cockpit. "Captain Oz, how about we make the Wally run? We want to ditch that speedboat."

Oz grinned. "'I feel the need . . . the need for speed,'" he said.

"Finally, somebody else who talks in movie quotes," Adam cheered. "*Top Gun*, baby!"

Oz gave him a thumbs-up and hit the throttle. The yacht shot forward, sprays of white foam in its wake. The wooden floor lurched beneath their feet. Jason instinctively grabbed Sienna by the waist and Belle by the arm, steadying them.

"No, no, don't worry about me," Adam muttered—

from the floor. He'd face-planted when the Wally jumped forward. "I can take care of myself." Adam used both hands to shove himself back to his feet.

"Sorry, guy, I only have two hands and I had to make a choice," Jason said. "Not that it was a difficult one," he added, grinning at Sienna and Belle.

"You were like a rock," Belle said. "You didn't even stumble."

"All that time on the surfboard must have paid off," Jason answered.

"Your boyfriend's useful," Belle told her friend. "I think you should keep him."

Sienna grinned and snuggled closer to Jason, but he was distracted by the speedboat. It had managed to catch up with them and was keeping pace. Goatee and his friend waved and smiled.

"They must have done some serious tinkering with that engine," Oz commented, frowning. "But the Wally has a CODOG propulsion system, and we're nowhere near full power." He let the clutch out. "I'm switching to the jet engines."

The speedboat stayed with them. Goatee raised his beer can in a toast.

Oz's lips tightened. "Okay. Forget tinkering, they must have replaced the engine altogether! But they don't know what they're up against." He flicked a few switches.

The speedboat kept pace for a moment, then began to fall behind.

Jason and Sienna cheered. "Bye, losers!" Belle yelled, even though there was no way the guys could hear her.

Oz grinned, satisfied.

"I'm going to grab a soda," Adam said, unsmiling. "You want one, Jason?" He shot Jason a look that Jason easily interpreted as Adam needing to talk to him—alone.

"Uh, sure," Jason said. "We'll serve you," he told Sienna and Belle.

He and Adam headed down to the lounge, where there was a refrigerator stocked with cold drinks. "What's up?" Jason asked.

Adam pulled a Coke out of the cooler and popped the top. He absently flicked the metal tab back and forth for a moment, trying to decide what to say.

"Come on, what's on your mind?" Jason prompted.

"That speedboat was really tricked out," Adam said.

"And?"

"And it would have taken some serious, serious bucks to do it. That boat shouldn't have been able to keep up with the Wally at all. And the scopes and cameras they were using? I know you didn't see them, but trust me. That stuff is not exactly standard-issue,"

Adam went on. "I think that maybe those guys weren't just . . . guys."

"You mean they were . . . *rich* guys?" Jason joked, but he felt his belly go cold. He was pretty sure he knew where Adam was headed with this.

"I didn't want to say anything in front of Belle, but I think there's a possibility that those guys are hunters. Tamburo-type hunters. The last time I searched 'vampire hunter' on the web, there was this billionaire who was offering a two-million-dollar reward for anyone who bagged a vampire," Adam said.

"Unbelievable," Jason muttered.

"It could be total bull," Adam replied. "The Net is full of trash. But . . ."

"Yeah." Jason leaned close to the huge windows of the lounge and peered out at the stretch of ocean behind them. "They're gone for now, at least."

"But we—"

"Hey, Adam, are we going to watch *Heathers* or not?" Belle called from the cockpit.

"On my way," he called back. He turned to Jason. "Like you said, they're gone now. We'll just have to keep our eyes open, see if they show up again." Jason nodded. "For now, the giant plasma—and Belle—are calling my name," Adam said. He took off for the stateroom. Belle went with him.

Sienna joined Jason in the lounge. "Weren't we in

the middle of something too?" she asked in a throaty voice.

"I think I was in the middle of my Snickers pie," Jason joked.

"Well, if you'd rather eat than dance with—" Sienna began.

"No," Jason interrupted her. "No, no, *no*." He took her hand, and they walked back out on deck, pausing by the CD player for Sienna to get their song playing again. The Wally powered on as they began to dance, the ride smooth even though they were up to almost fifty knots. Glimmering blue-green water all around them. Hot sun on their shoulders. The teakwood deck rocking gently beneath their feet. *Nothing better,* Jason decided as he wrapped his arms around Sienna's waist, pulling her closer, her silky hair brushing against his cheek, the curves of her body warm against him. *Absolutely nothing better.* He'd be happy to stay here, in this moment, for the entire next year.

But the yacht suddenly gave a sharp turn, ruining their dance. A moment later, footsteps sounded on the stairs leading belowdecks. "Did we hit an iceberg or what?" Adam asked as he and Belle emerged on deck.

Sienna frowned, looking around. "We turned back toward shore."

"We're heading home?" Belle asked. "Adam and I

barely started the movie. I thought we were staying out for a few more hours."

"We are. I told Oz we wanted to be on the water for the sunset," Sienna said. "I'll go check with him." She headed for the cockpit. Jason tagged along to see what the deal was.

"Hey, Captain!" Sienna called when they reached Oz. "What's going on? The sun doesn't go down for hours."

Oz gave an apologetic shrug. "Your father just radioed me. He said I had to get you back."

"Why?" Sienna demanded.

"No explanation given," Oz told her. "He just said to return to the marina immediately. And he didn't sound happy."

"Great. Just great!" Sienna fumed, her dark eyes blazing. Jason got the feeling *she* wasn't happy either.

FOUR

"What's the deal?" Belle asked when Sienna and Jason returned to the deck.

"My dad ordered us back in," Sienna explained, her voice filled with anger.

"Why?" Belle exclaimed.

"He didn't give Oz a reason, but . . ." Sienna glanced at Jason.

"Oh," Belle said.

"Oh?" Jason repeated. "What does that mean? Am I missing something?"

Sienna looked away, biting her lip.

"Did he know who we were out here with?" Belle asked.

"I just told him you and a couple of other friends," Sienna admitted. "Which he should have no problem with. Brad and I used the yacht tons of times."

"Oh," Jason said again. He got it now. The difference between him and Brad? Brad was a vampire. Jason, not so much.

"I thought it was supposed to be the other way around," Adam joked. "I thought the *human* parents were supposed to disapprove of their kids dating the undead."

Sienna and Belle stared at him.

"Is 'undead' not the PC term?" Adam asked. "I just meant . . . vampires. They don't even usually have parents around. Angel—no parents. Dracula—no parents. Not that they didn't have parents at some point, but their parents have usually all been dead for . . ." Adam shoved his hands through his shaggy sand-colored hair. "I'm making it so much worse, right?"

"Right," Jason told him.

"I'll shut up now," Adam volunteered.

Belle laughed and patted his arm. "I get the verbal diarrhea sometimes too."

"Who I'm with might not even be the issue," Sienna said. "Maybe Dad got his credit card bill. I did spend a teensy bit more on that Balenciaga bag than my approved clothing allowance for the month."

"Would he really be so pissed about the bill that he'd have the captain turn the boat around?" Jason asked dubiously.

"I don't know. But I'm going to find out," Sienna seethed. "My father's spoiled everything!"

She hardly looked at Jason—or Belle or Adam—on the way back. As soon as the yacht pulled into the marina, she stormed down the gangplank onto the pier. Then she turned and blew Jason a kiss. "Sorry. I know I've been awful," she called. "I just need to get this straightened out."

Sienna turned and headed down the boardwalk, her dark hair whipping in the breeze.

Belle rushed after her. "Bye, guys!" she called over her shoulder.

Jason and Adam stared after them for a moment. Then Adam turned to Jason. "Thanks for inviting me. I had a lovely time," he said solemnly. They both cracked up as they walked down the gangplank.

"I hope Sienna's dad is ticked about the shopping and not about my, you know, being a human," Jason said as they walked past a couple of more ordinary-looking yachts.

"I believe the word you're searching for is 'humanity,'" Adam said. "Or possibly 'humanosity.' Or is it 'humanaliciousness'?"

Jason just looked at him.

"Oh. We're being serious," Adam said. "Okay, well, maybe he just found out Sienna was socializing with somebody from the wrong side of the DeVere Heights gates. You and Belle are acceptable company. But me?"

"Yeah, the slums of Malibu, where you live, are known to produce some pretty dangerous characters," Jason said.

Adam grinned. "But seriously. Really seriously—

your parents would probably not be so happy if they knew you were going out with a V, am I right?"

"You mean after their parental heads exploded?" Jason answered. "It's not so much the going-out part as the vampires-existing part that would, uh, agitate them."

"Good point," Adam agreed. They climbed down the pier steps and started across the beach. "When I first put the whole vampire situation together, I was freaked. Now I spend part of every day researching vampire hunters like it's totally normal adolescent behavior. I mean, I hardly ever get time to even look at MySpace these days. I'm just too busy doing searches on vampire killers."

"It's a good thing you are, though," Jason said. "You're right about us needing to stay watchful. I wanted to think Tamburo was an aberration, but we can't be sure of that."

"So I'll keep doing the research, and we'll both keep our eyes peeled for any weirdness. Any weirdness that isn't our regular DeVere Heights weirdness, that is," Adam clarified.

"Right." Jason pulled out his cell. "How long before I can call Sienna and find out what the deal is?"

"Ten minutes for her to drive home—unless the Spider gets temperamental. Then a parental fight—mine usually last from two minutes to an hour and a half, and girls are more verbal than boys," Adam hesitated, calculating. "I'd say you need to give her at least two hours. More, if you want to factor in some recovery time, which I would."

"Okay, so what are we going to do for the next two hours or so? I need distracting," Jason told his friend.

"Pool table? McGuire's?" Adam suggested. "I could whip your butt a few times?"

"Pool table. McGuire's," Jason agreed. "And maybe I'll let you beat me once."

Three games later—all lost by Jason—Adam replaced his cue in the rack at McGuire's. "Call her already," he told Jason. "You're at an hour fifty-four. And you suck so bad that winning has lost almost all meaning for me."

Jason pulled out his cell and hit speed dial. After three rings, Sienna's voice mail picked up. "Hi, this is Sienna. Do what you've got to do when you hear the beep."

"Hey, it's me," Jason said into the phone. "Just checking in to see if you've been nabbed by the shoe police. Call me."

He tried Sienna again before dinner. Same deal.

And after dinner.

And before he went to bed. Same old, same old.

After he'd lain in bed for an hour, not being able to sleep, he tried her one more time. No Sienna. Just her voice mail message. What was going on?

• • •

"What's going on? What happened yesterday?" Jason asked Sienna when he caught her at her locker between second and third period the next day. This semester they didn't have any classes together except European history—last of the day.

Sienna rolled her eyes. "Parents." She slammed her locker door. "I'm almost eighteen. I'll be in college this year. And they're trying to tell me how I should spend my time!"

"So it wasn't about the clothes?" Jason asked, even though he already knew the answer.

"They didn't like it that you and I were out on the yacht together. They acted like it was some kind of floating motel or something. I mean, yes, it has bedrooms, but we were hardly alone. And it's not like the yacht is the only place we could . . . if we were doing that. We could be doing it in your car, for all they know."

"The Bug is a little small," Jason joked, trying to lighten the mood. "We'll figure something out. Maybe I could talk to them, or you could invite me for family dinner or something."

Sienna smiled. "We'll strategize tonight. We're still going to the movies, right?"

"Definitely," Jason promised as the warning bell rang.

Sienna gave him a quick kiss. "Can't wait," she said.

• • •

Jason couldn't wait until it was time to leave that evening. He had a little more than an hour. He headed to the bathroom for a hair check. He spotted Dani coming down the hall from the opposite direction. "Just give me one second before—"

Too late. Dani had slipped into the bathroom in front of him. "You better go downstairs. I have a lot of girly stuff to do," she told him. "I'm going out."

"I'm going out too," Jason complained. "And it'll take me less than five minutes."

"All my makeup and everything is in here." Dani tossed him his hairbrush and deodorant. "There. You're good to go. Use a different bathroom." She shut the door.

"Guys don't care that much about makeup anyway," Jason advised. "So your hot date or whatever isn't even going to notice."

"Guys like you don't notice," Dani answered. "Other guys do."

"Who is this enlightened guy, anyway?" Jason asked.

"I don't want to talk about it." Dani opened the door a crack and peered at Jason. "I like him . . . a lot. And I'm pretty sure he likes me. I don't want to mess it up by talking about it. It always messes things up if you talk about them too much."

"I doubt this guy has the bathroom bugged. If he does, you have bigger problems to worry about," Jason told her.

"I'm getting in the shower now, so if you keep talking, you're going to be talking to yourself," Dani announced, closing the door again.

"Fine," Jason muttered. He took his brush and deodorant and headed back to his room, wondering about the guy Dani liked so much. He hadn't noticed her hanging around with any one particular guy at school. But she had gone to the movies with Ryan Patrick that time. Well, Ryan and a bunch of her other friends. Was Ryan the guy his sister was falling for?

Ryan did make a point of telling me to invite Dani to his Valentine's Day party, Jason remembered. *So maybe Ryan is falling for Dani, too.*

Jason wasn't crazy about that idea. Not when he was almost positive that Ryan had fangs. Jason didn't have anything against the vampires. How could he? He was totally, insanely in love with one of them. But he knew it could be dangerous to be around them. Hell, it was dangerous just to know they existed! Jason had almost been killed twice since he'd learned the truth about the popular crowd at DeVere High.

But Dani couldn't be in love with a vampire, Jason told himself. Not yet, anyway. Ryan—if Ryan was even the guy she'd been gushing over—had only been back in school for a few months. Surely that wasn't long enough for Dani to get really serious about him.

Yeah, like you didn't fall for Sienna the first time you saw her, a voice in Jason's head mocked. *That first day at school, in the cafeteria line, when she teased you for being clueless about what a green Borba was—you were gone. Do you think Dani is so—*

Jason was pulled out of his thoughts by the sound of a text message arriving on his cell. The message was from Sienna: "Got to go to charity thing with the rents. Sorry, sorry, sorry. Talk in the a.m. XXOO."

Unbelievable.

Or else totally believable and just a continuation of what had happened yesterday on the yacht. *Have Sienna's parents decided to try and keep her from seeing me?* Jason wondered.

Jason took a deep breath. He couldn't let himself get all bent about this until he knew for sure what the deal was. Sienna's parents were really into the local charity scene. Maybe Sienna had just forgotten about one of the million events her parents expected her to attend. Maybe it was just a coincidence that this was happening the day after Mr. Devereux had ordered the yacht back to shore.

Jason flopped down on his bed and kicked off his shoes, then flipped on the TV. He should probably study, but he was so not in the mood. He channel surfed all the way up to the pay-per-view stuff and all the way back down again. Nothing held his attention for more than a few seconds.

Finally, with a growl of frustration, he gave up and snatched his chemistry book off the nightstand. He might as well get something slightly worthwhile out of his evening, even if it was just a few more points on the next chem quiz.

The thing was, four hours later, when he heard Dani coming up the stairs, he couldn't remember a thing that he'd read. He hadn't really been able to stop thinking about Sienna.

Jason couldn't stop himself from grinning, though, when he heard Dani singing as she walked by his room. *At least somebody had a good time,* he thought. He leaned over to switch off his bedside lamp and a twinge of pain vibrated through his chest muscles where the crossbow had wounded him.

The grin slid off his face. If Dani had been hanging with Ryan a few months ago, she could have been the one who'd ended up with a crossbow bolt in her chest. *It's dangerous for her to get involved with any of the vampires,* Jason thought. *Life-and-death dangerous.*

FIVE

Sienna gave a little beep on the Spider's horn as Jason walked through the school parking lot the next morning. He hurried over and swung himself into the passenger seat, leaning in for a kiss before he'd even closed the door.

But Sienna's grave expression stopped him. "What's wrong?" he asked, brushing her long hair away from her face.

"My parents sat me down for a *talk* when we got home from that charity dinner last night," she said. "They don't want me to see you anymore."

"What?" Horror rocked through Jason's body.

"I know." Sienna sounded miserable.

"But I don't get it. What's changed?" Jason asked. "It's not like we've been hiding the fact that we're together. I'm over at your house all the time. Your parents seemed fine with it."

"I know. I thought my parents liked you, even," Sienna answered. "And they do. They kept saying that last night. They think you're a really good person. They are so grateful to you for the way you went after Tamburo when he was going to kill me. They know you saved my life, but . . ." her voice trailed off.

"But I'm not a *vampire*!" The statement came out harder than Jason had meant it to, fueled by frustration and sadness.

"Yeah." Sienna stroked his arm. "Yeah."

"I still don't understand why they suddenly want you to break up with me. It's not like they ever thought I *was* a vampire," Jason pointed out. "It's not new information."

"I know. I said the same thing," Sienna told him. "Basically, they didn't think you and I were ever going to get that serious. They figured that if they just left the situation alone, time would take care of the problem."

Jason ran his hand through his hair. "Problem," he repeated. "And what exactly *is* the problem? Did they say?" Jason asked. "If we knew exactly what they were thinking, maybe we could find a way to change their minds."

Sienna let out a sigh that seemed to come from the very depths of her soul. "They just kept telling me that there were too many risks. They don't think it's safe for me—or for you, either."

Jason took a moment and forced himself to consider things from her parents' point of view. "Okay. I get how there are risks for me," he said. "Like Tamburo coming after me because he thought I was a . . . one of you. But I'm willing to take whatever risks there are. I want to be with you, no matter what." He shook his head. "What I don't understand is why your parents think going out with a human is any kind of risk for you."

"I think they finally realized we're really in love," Sienna told him.

"And that should be a good thing, right?" Jason asked.

"It should be. No it *is*," Sienna said, her voice cracking a little. "But now that they've really accepted that, I think they're afraid that we're going to want to be together forever."

"And what if we do?" Jason demanded.

"Forever. Like *hundreds of years*," Sienna explained. "Which would mean me making you a vampire. Turning you. And that's forbidden. By the DeVere Heights Vampire Council *and* the Vampire High Council."

"What about my aunt? She was turned," Jason argued.

"That was only allowed because her husband was so powerful. He was on the Vampire High Council. No one could stop him." Sienna took Jason's hand. "It's not about you and me. It's about humans and vampires. Transformation brings our two worlds together, and my parents—my parents and everyone else—think that's hugely dangerous for all vampires. And for humans, too."

"So transformation is the big problem. Okay. So we go to your parents and we promise them that that won't happen," Jason said, staring intently into Sienna's eyes. He could see that she wasn't convinced he'd found a solution.

"There's something else," she admitted after a moment's hesitation. "And this is what *they* think. It's not what *I* think. . . ."

Jason nodded.

"They think another vampire is always going to be better at keeping our secrets, because they share the same secrets," Sienna tried to explain.

Jason could feel anger welling up inside him. Sienna's parents thought he couldn't be trusted not to expose them just because he was a human? Even after everything he'd been through in order to protect their vampire secrets.

"I would never do anything that could possibly hurt you. Or your parents. Or any of you. Haven't I proved that?" he demanded. "After stopping Tamburo? After being attacked by Luke Archer when he was consumed by the bloodlust, and *not* going to the cops—or even to my own parents!" He slammed his fist on the dashboard.

Sienna winced.

"Sorry," Jason told her. "I know it's not what *you* think. But your parents are way out of line."

"Jason. My parents think that the DeVere Heights Vampire Council might even decide to take some action—against both of us—if they find out how serious we are about each other. I don't know if they're right or not. No vampire has gotten really involved with a human for as long as I can remember. I'm not sure what the Council would do if they thought . . . well, if they thought our whole community was in danger of being exposed."

Jason stared blankly out at the parking lot, trying to absorb this new information. He'd watched the DeVere Heights Vampire Council discuss his friend Tyler Deegan's fate. He'd seen them talking about Tyler as if his life were theirs to take if they wanted to. Half the members had wanted Tyler put to death— even though he didn't have a clue that they were vampires. He was no real threat to them. He'd stolen from them, true, but he couldn't really hurt them.

What would the Council do to Sienna if they thought she was endangering all of her kind?

"So I really am a risk to you," he said slowly. "I don't want you brought before the DeVere Heights Vampire Council because of me. But we need a plan. There has to be some way to prove to your parents— and the Council—that I'm trustworthy."

"My parents aren't going to change their minds," Sienna answered. "And they would have a mutual meltdown if they thought we were going to try to talk to the Council." She fell silent, and suddenly Jason realized what had just happened. She'd said it was over. She'd broken up with him. The truth slammed into him like a killer wave.

Sienna locked eyes with him. "But I'm not giving you up. I'm not."

Jason laughed, relief spiraling through his body. "That's good to hear."

"We'll just have to act like we're going along with my parents," Sienna said thoughtfully. "So, no making out in front of your locker," she went on with a grin.

"Or in my car. Or in the cafeteria line. Or in European history," Jason added.

"Yeah, because I'm always making out with you in the middle of class," Sienna teased.

"You know you want to." Jason laughed. "So, we keep things secret?"

Sienna nodded. "At school we act like we broke up but stayed friends. We only talk to each other if there's at least one other person around. And we don't even do that too much; you know how everyone gossips at this school. Plus, and I hate to say it about my own, but vampires gossip worse than anybody."

"Yeah, I've seen that grapevine in action." Jason laughed.

"Starting now, we go underground," Sienna said with an emphatic nod.

"So after *this*, we go underground," Jason corrected, pressing his lips against hers.

He had meant the kiss to be short, fast, sneaky. But the taste of her, the soft warmth of her lips, made it hard to pull away. Sienna was addictive. No doubt.

"This whole 'not talking to each other too much' thing is going to be tough," he told her at last.

"Complete torture," Sienna agreed. "We have to meet up tonight."

"Where?" Jason asked, already mentally sorting through the possibilities.

"Someplace no one goes," Sienna answered. "But now we have to move. Looks like the first bell already rang." She nodded toward the people suddenly streaming into the mission-style main building of DeVere High. "We'll have to figure it out later."

"Okay. We'll text." Jason took her hand and brought it to his mouth. "And we'll ignore each other."

Sienna's breath quickened as he kissed her palm. "That won't be easy," she murmured.

Jason reluctantly let go of her. When she'd hurried into the school, he climbed out of the car and walked into the building alone. As if they'd broken up. He strode down the crowded hallway, telling himself not to miss Sienna. This was what they had to do to keep the fact that they were still a couple a secret.

He wasn't going to do anything that could bring the Council down on her. He loved her too much.

"5. Under pier. La Costa Beach," Sienna texted him between first and second period.

"Swim practice. Sux. Srry." Jason texted back.

"8. Movie about the math genius? No 1 we know will see that," he suggested in another text message between second and third.

"Auction for some worthy thing. Parents insist. Sux," Sienna instantly answered.

"Mdnght. Ftball field. Bleachers???" Jason offered in his next message as he got in the food line at lunch. Only Brad and two guys from the diving team separated him from Sienna. But Jason didn't want to risk talking to her. Not on day one of Operation Secret Couple.

"If caught sneaking in, grounded 4 life," Sienna answered by text.

"B4 skool a.m. Bad dnut place?" Jason shot back.

"Tomorrow? But it's tomorrow!" Sienna replied. "Can't w8 that long."

Jason laughed and shook his head at his phone. Then he typed, "Skipping swimming. See U under pier."

Sienna glanced over her shoulder and smiled at him by way of reply.

• • •

Jason checked his watch as he sat on the beach wait-ing for Sienna after school. He'd been waiting for more than an hour under the beat-up fishing pier. Had something gone wrong? Had her parents found out about their plans somehow? The vampire grapevine couldn't be *that* good. Could it?

Sienna's usually late, he reminded himself. She ran on girl time, the same way Dani and his aunt Bianca did.

He looked around and noted with satisfaction that under a half-rotten pier, in February, with the sun about to go down was the perfect choice for an Operation Secret Couple meeting. Other than some fish and some seagulls, Jason seemed to be the only living creature for miles.

He checked his watch again. Sienna was seriously late. Even on girl time.

The sky looked as if it were on fire over to the west as the blazing red ball of the sun got ready to hit the water. *Sienna should be here to witness this,* Jason thought. It was one of the best sunsets he'd seen since he'd moved to Malibu.

He pulled out his cell to text Sienna. Before he'd got-ten two letters in, he heard a creaking sound above him.

Jason froze.

Rotten wood creaks, he told himself. But he kept his body motionless, waiting for another sound.

Creak!

Footsteps? Jason wondered. *Sienna?* But they'd agreed to meet under the pier, not on it.

Jason slowly stretched out on his back. He stared up at the warped planks that made up the pier. Shafts of light filtered through each space between the planks. But with the next creak, some of that light was blocked.

The creaks were definitely footsteps. Somebody was up on the pier. And it wasn't Sienna.

Jason felt his heart start to race. He'd been on the beach when Tamburo shot him with a crossbow bolt. On the beach, alone, at sunset. Just like now. And Adam thought there might be more hunters around. Was a vampire-hunter up on the old pier now, looking for him? Or, worse, *looking for Sienna?*

Jason flipped onto his stomach and combat-crawled down the beach toward the surf. When he got to the end of the pier, he put one foot in the V of a support beam and swung himself up to take a quick scan of the pier.

Goatee guy from the speedboat was walking in his direction, looking about him as if searching for someone. He certainly didn't seem to have Sienna. Jason ducked his head, determined to keep out of sight. *You're in the perfect spot,* he told himself, wrapping both arms around the beam. *Even if he looks under the pier, he won't see you unless he circles around and actually stands in the surf.*

Jason held his position until his arms ached and his legs started to cramp, then he allowed himself another quick look over the edge of the pier. It was empty now. Cautiously, he pulled himself up onto the rough planks. In the last bit of light from the sunset, he saw a black Mercedes race away down the Pacific Coast Highway.

When it was out of sight, he pulled out his cell and dialed Sienna.

"Sorry. I couldn't get there," Sienna's voice filled his ear, low and breathless. "I'm helping Mom unload the floral arrangements for the auction. She'll be back any second. I'm stuck here. She insists she needs my help setting up because someone got sick or something."

Jason's galloping heartbeat began to slow. Sienna was okay. If Goatee was a hunter, he hadn't found his prey. "You think your mom knows we were planning to meet?" Jason asked, choosing not to tell Sienna about Goatee; he didn't want to terrify her until he knew what was going on.

"I guess it's possible," Sienna whispered. "But I don't know. She and Dad might just be trying to pack my schedule so full that there's no way we can sneak off somewhere. My father actually signed me up to play in a father-daughter golf tournament this weekend. And I so don't golf!"

"Then when—"

"My mom's coming back. I gotta go," Sienna muttered, and hung up.

Jason slowly folded his phone. Then he sat and stared at the sky until all the color had drained away and the beach and the pier and even the waves were all shades of gray. *Is this how it's going to be?* he couldn't stop himself from wondering. *Is this going to keep happening?*

Is this the end for me and Sienna?

SIX

Jason headed up to his car . . . and sat there, his mind shifting back and forth between the Sienna situation and the strangeness of Goatee showing up at the pier.

Out of the corner of his eye he caught a flash of movement down on the beach. Goatee guy? Had he circled back?

Jason squinted into the shadows by the pier. The figure looked too tall to be either of the guys from the speedboat. The hair looked too dark. . . .

The figure moved out of the shadows. It was Brad.

What was he doing down there? Nobody from school came to La Costa Beach. That was the whole point of Jason and Sienna meeting there. Jason noticed that Brad was carrying fishing gear. The silhouette of the pole was pretty easy to make out. Jason hadn't been fishing since he moved to Malibu. Maybe this was supposed to be a good spot for it. It kind of made sense, with the old pier and everything.

He watched as Brad continued down the beach and then started cutting up the side of the cliff to the highway. Jason realized that Brad's car was parked farther down the road on the opposite side from Jason's. It definitely hadn't been there when Jason arrived.

Jason put his key in the ignition and started the Bug. He wanted to get out of here. If Brad noticed him, he might come over. And Jason didn't want to have to come up with a reason for what he himself was doing there.

He started the car, then impulsively turned right on PCH instead of left. He wasn't ready to go home. He'd only end up staring blankly at the tube or wasting time studying when his retention capacity was a complete zero. He'd drop by Adam's instead.

"Jason, hey," Adam's father said when he opened the front door. "You came on the right night. I just made my ten-alarm chili." The guy was wearing an apron that said BACON IS A VEGETABLE on the front. Jason was starting to feel a little better already. "Adam's eating in his room," Sheriff Turnball continued. "I couldn't pry him away from his computer. Grab yourself a bowlful from the pot on the stove and go on up."

"Cool. Thanks." Jason obediently headed into the kitchen. Just the smell of the chili made his eyes and nose start to water. *What is this stuff gonna do to my stomach lining?* he wondered, serving himself up a big bowlful nonetheless. How could you turn down chow made by somebody with a BACON IS A VEGETABLE apron? Then he made his way to Adam's room.

"Oh, man, you came on the wrong night," Adam told him from his seat in front of the computer. "Ten-alarm chili is dangerous."

Jason flopped down on Adam's unmade bed and caught sight of the image on his computer screen. "Is that a *chicken* drinking that woman's blood?" he sputtered.

"It's one of the Vampire Chickens of Borneo, according to the *believe* website," Adam replied. "Me, I'm inclined not to *believe*. Even I draw the line somewhere, and that somewhere is bloodsucking poultry."

"You haven't seen any more info on that reward for killing vampires, have you?" Jason asked.

"I checked that site again after we got followed by our friends in the speedboat," Adam answered. "A few people had posted messages on the bulletin board: exchanging vampire kill methods, asking if anyone had spotted any of the undead—that kind of thing."

"Anyone mention Malibu?" Jason asked.

His friend spun his desk chair around so he was facing Jason. "Okay, tell Uncle Adam. What's going on?"

"Sienna and I were supposed to meet under that old pier on La Costa Beach this evening."

"Romantic! The smell of mold, the thrilling possibility that you'll die together as the pier collapses on top of you," Adam commented. "So what happened?"

"Sienna didn't show. Her mom made her go early to some charity auction. But I saw the goateed dude from the speedboat."

"Did he see you?" Adam demanded quickly.

Jason shook his head. "I managed to stay out of sight."

"Good." For once, Adam sounded serious. "We don't need you to get shot by another vampire hunter. And Sienna had a close call last time too. I'm kinda glad her mom kept her out of commission tonight."

"Yeah," Jason said. "I'm glad she wasn't there when Goatee came sniffing around. And later I saw Brad. Wouldn't that have been fun—me and Sienna and her ex, watching the sunset together?"

Adam raised one eyebrow. "Brad showed up? That's . . . interesting," he commented.

"I did think it was a little strange that he was there," Jason admitted. "But he had a fishing pole. People fish there, right?"

"People used to fish from the pier all the time, before it started falling apart," Adam answered. "I'm sure people still fish around there, but . . ." He did the one-eyebrow thing again.

"Can you use actual words to say whatever it is you're trying to say? Instead of attempting to communicate with your facial hair?" Jason demanded.

"Okay, okay. But I don't know if I even have anything to say," Adam answered. "Maybe I'm just going all Son-of-a-Cop."

"Spit it out," Jason ordered.

"Well, you might want to consider the possibility that Brad is keeping his eye on you and Sienna. Maybe even feeding intel to Sienna's parents," Adam said.

"I did think that maybe Sienna's parents had found out we were meeting, and that that was why the whole charity thing had come up," Jason admitted. "But Brad? That makes no sense. Brad said he was cool with me and Sienna getting together. He even said he and Sienna were better as friends," Jason protested.

"Again, Son-of-a-Cop here," Adam put in. "But people do this thing sometimes. . . . It's called ly-ing." Adam said the last few words in a whisper.

Jason shook his head. "Why would Brad lie? Why bother?"

"Pride maybe," Adam offered. "It was clear Sienna wanted to be with you, so it was less embarrassing for him to act like he was pretty much done with her, at least in a romantic way."

A fragment of memory flashed through Jason's mind. He and Sienna texting each other at lunch. Brad in the lunch line between them. Could he have read the text messages over Sienna's shoulder?

Still, they were talking about Brad here. Pretty

much the most decent guy Jason knew. "I don't buy it," he told Adam. "But I guess I should keep an eye on him. I'm more worried about Sienna's parents, though. They're the ones who could really mess things up between me and Sienna." Jason started to spoon some chili into his mouth.

"Really. Don't eat it," Adam warned, watching him. "Those wasabi peas I had at your place? Jelly beans compared to that stuff."

Jason felt his eyes begin to water as the chili came closer. He hadn't even put any in his mouth yet. Maybe Adam was right. He put the spoon back and set the bowl down on Adam's nightstand. "So what am I supposed to do?"

Adam pulled an energy bar out of one of his desk drawers. "Eat this. It's not a great dinner, but—"

"What am I supposed to do about *Sienna and her parents*, doofus?" Jason demanded, unwrapping the bar anyway.

"I don't think her parents should be making calls about who she goes out with," Adam said slowly. "That's messed up . . ."

"But?" Jason prompted.

"I didn't say 'but,'" Adam protested.

"Yeah, but it was there anyway. Out with it," Jason urged.

"I've been reading a lot of stuff about vampires,

ever since I started getting suspicious about our, you know, special friends. And now, with trying to find out what other kinds of vampire-hunting freaks we might need to know about . . ."

Jason circled his hands in the air in a come-on, come-on gesture.

"Well, basically, there's a lot of tragic crap that goes down when vampires and humans hook up. Like the whole aging thing. I mean, I'm guessing Sienna and her crowd live a lot longer than we do, if not forever. Am I right?" Adam asked.

"Yeah. From what Sienna told me, they aren't immortal, but they can live for centuries," Jason confirmed.

"So at some point, you'll be this old man, and Sienna will be . . ." Adam let his sentence trail off.

"Still young and hot," Jason finished for him.

"So, hey, you could be like Michael Douglas to her Catherine Zeta-Jones. Not a bad way to go," Adam joked, but his eyes were solemn.

"It's really hard to worry about what's going to happen years from now. I probably should, but right now all I can think about is how I'm going to see her *today*, you know?" Jason took a bite of the energy bar. Stale.

Adam nodded. "And you're already okay with her having to drink blood. That's the other biggie."

"It doesn't thrill me," Jason confessed. "I mean, I understand that she has to do it. But it's a little weird, when you stop and think about it."

"A *little* weird?" Adam grinned. "You've been in Malibu too long, my man. Most people would consider the drinking of the blood a *lot* weird. But what about the bit where she has to make out with other guys to get it?"

"That was hard, at first," Jason confessed. "But I'm used to it now. Hey look, I love Sienna. She needs blood to live. Therefore I want her to drink blood. It's simple. I just have to accept that every few days she's going to have to make out with another guy."

"Would it help if she drank exclusively from a friend, someone you like and admire? Say, Adam Turnball? Because your baby—she's hot."

"Thanks. That was an image I really needed to have in my head," Jason sighed.

Adam laughed. "Sorry. Just pulling your chain."

"Somehow I don't think Dani would be okay with her boyfriend making out with other girls, though," Jason said thoughtfully.

"Whoa. Brain whiplash. Dani? Huh?" Adam asked.

"I think Dani might be into Ryan Patrick. They might even have gone out the other night," Jason explained. "If anyone should be cool with it, it's me.

But it kinda freaks me out. What if someone goes after Dani with a crossbow?" He gave a groan of frustration. "I sound like Sienna's parents."

"No, I can see why you're worried about Dani," Adam said. "It's better if they never get things started. That way they'll never end up in the situation you and Sienna are in."

"But I wouldn't want to go back and warn myself not to fall for Sienna. If time travel were possible and all that," Jason answered. "Whatever the risks, it's worth it. *She's* worth it."

"I think—"

Jason's cell beeped, interrupting Adam. "That's a text. Maybe it's Sienna," Jason said, pulling his cell out of his pocket.

"Is it?" Adam asked.

"Nope. It's my mom, calling me home for dinner," Jason said, deflated.

"Look on the bright side. You're probably not having ten-alarm chili," Adam consoled him.

Jason took a bite of his peach cobbler and tried to focus on what his mother was saying instead of thinking about Sienna.

"I've left three messages for my sister in the last week and a half, and she still hasn't called me back," Mrs. Freeman was complaining.

"Maybe she's out of town," Mr. Freeman suggested.

Yeah, out of town on vampire business, Jason thought. Aunt Bianca was high up in the vampire—he wasn't sure what to call it—the vampire political scene. He'd seen her take charge of the DeVere Heights Vampire Council.

She hadn't seen him, though. Jason still wasn't sure what would have happened to him if she had.

"According to her assistant, she *is* away," Mrs. Freeman agreed. "But how is that any excuse? You know she calls in to the office every day, which means she's got my messages."

"Where's Aunt Bianca this time?" Dani asked eagerly. She was fascinated by her aunt. She'd already decided that she wanted to be a casting agent like Bianca someday. And have a house on each coast. And a huge walk-in closet on both coasts to hold all her fabulous designer wear.

"Who knows?' Mrs. Freeman snapped. "Even her assistant isn't sure. Bianca calls, barks out some orders to Jacinda, and hangs up."

"Maybe she's in Paris," Dani suggested. "Paris is supposed to be awesome."

According to Ryan Patrick, recently returned from a semester in Paris, Jason thought.

"Maybe," Mrs. Freeman said. "Jacinda did say that on one of Bianca's latest calls she insisted that from then on they always answer the phone at the office in French. I think even Jacinda's becoming concerned about her erratic behavior."

"Your sister has never been exactly predictable, Tania," Mr. Freeman reminded her.

"True." Jason's mom stared down at her dessert plate. "True, but predictable isn't the same as weird. The French thing is just weird."

"I don't think it's so weird," Dani said. "Maybe Bianca wants them to speak French because it reminds her of Uncle Stefan."

"But why now?" Mrs. Freeman asked. "Stefan has been dead for almost two years."

"Delayed reaction, maybe," Dani suggested, but even she sounded doubtful. "Maybe it's suddenly hit her that he's gone forever and she just really misses him."

"Maybe." Mrs. Freeman sighed, frowning. "But that doesn't quite ring true to me. I can't shake the feeling that something is wrong with Bianca. Really wrong."

A quick triple knock sounded on the front door.

"That could be Bianca now," Mr. Freeman suggested. "She's got all your messages, she's in L.A., and she decided to drop by. She loves the drop-by, your sister."

"I'll get it," Jason volunteered. If it was his aunt,

he wanted the chance to sound her out in private and find out if she was the one who had restocked his college account.

He swung the door open—and time seemed to stand still. Every thought about his aunt Bianca, his money, everything . . . disappeared.

She stood there. In a strapless crimson dress. Her dark hair cascading over her bare shoulders.

Sienna.

SEVEN

"Wow," Jason breathed. "You look incredible."

Sienna smiled, her lipstick the same crimson as her long dress. "Incredible enough for you to invite me in before someone sees me?"

"Oh yeah, of course." Jason stepped back to let her in. "My parents and Dani are finishing dinner. Let's go upstairs, where we can talk."

Sienna nodded. Jason grabbed her hand and led her up to his bedroom. "Sienna's here, you guys. Somebody finish my dessert," he called down the stairs, realizing he'd forgotten to say who was at the door.

"I'll handle that," his dad called back.

"I can only stay for a minute," Sienna told him once he'd shut the door behind them. "Belle and I got permission to leave the auction early. I'm supposed to be over at her house studying. Her dad's home, and he will definitely report in to my parents if I show up later than he thinks I should. I told Belle not to go straight inside, to buy us a little time."

Sienna started to pace back and forth across the room. "I should have just called. Or texted. But I wanted to see your face. I wanted to tell you in person how sorry I am I stood you up today." Her eyes were bright with unshed tears.

"It's okay. I know you didn't want to." Jason stepped in front of her to stop her agitated pacing. He put his hands on her shoulders. "It's okay, Sienna."

"No, it's not. My parents somehow found out I was planning on meeting you," Sienna burst out.

Brad? Jason couldn't help wondering.

"That's why my mom made me help her set up the auction," Sienna continued. "I don't know how they found out, but they did. And they are so furious with me for going behind their backs." She gave a harsh laugh. "Or, at least, for *trying* to go behind their backs."

Jason felt a tremor run through her body, and he tried to wrap his arms around her. Sienna pulled back, holding him away from her. "Jason . . ." Her voice shook. "They told me since I can't be trusted, they don't want you and I to be alone together. At all. They realize that we have classes together, that we have the same friends and go to the same parties. They aren't saying that we can't be, like, in the same room. But if they hear that we're alone together, anywhere, ever, then . . ."

"Then?" Jason prompted.

"Then they're sending me to boarding school. In France." Sienna's lips tightened into a thin line. "I have an older cousin there. She and her husband will 'keep an eye' on me apparently. And I'd stay at their place when school's out."

Jason was speechless. How had things gotten so insane so fast? Just a few days ago he'd been hanging at Sienna's house, kissing her in her own room.

"Say something," Sienna urged.

"I-I can hardly believe this is happening. I keep trying to think of some way to fix it, but . . . ," Jason replied.

"But there isn't a way." Sienna sighed. "My parents aren't kidding around. And they don't give a lot of second chances. We get caught out one more time, and I'm going to France."

"No," Jason said firmly. "I couldn't take that—not being able to see you at all. We just have to . . . we have to stay away from each other."

Sienna shook her head. "No. I'm not letting them split us up. We'll just be careful. Extra careful. I don't know how they're getting their info on us, so for now let's just be as paranoid as we can possibly be." She glanced at the clock on his DVD player. "I've been here too long. I've got to get to Belle's. We'll talk tomorrow."

"In public," Jason reminded her.

"In public," Sienna agreed. "We'll figure this out."

"Definitely," Jason answered, although he had no clue how. They'd been pretty careful today, and Sienna's parents had still found out about their plans.

He led her downstairs to the front door. "So, I'll see you tomorrow," he said. He wanted to kiss her, but the front door had a long window that ran alongside it. Could someone be watching them even now?

"Tomorrow," Sienna agreed. She slipped out the door and vanished into the darkness.

Jason stared into the night for a long moment, then shut the door. He headed for the kitchen on autopilot. He might as well see if there was any cobbler left. Though it was doubtful. His dad loved cobbler.

"I don't know what it is about that girl," he heard his mother saying, just as he was about to step inside the room. "Even though I'm sure she's very nice, there's just something about her that makes me uneasy."

"Overprotective much, Mom?" Dani teased.

Mrs. Freeman laughed. "I expect I am. That's what happens when you love your kids."

If she knew the truth about Sienna, she'd be acting just the way Sienna's parents are, Jason realized. *She'd build a dungeon in the basement, or whatever it took, to keep us apart. What are we going to do?* he asked himself. *What the hell are we going to do?*

Suddenly, he couldn't stand still. Every nerve and muscle in his body was begging for release. He didn't bother to change. He was already wearing his sneakers, that was good enough. "I'm going out for a run," he announced, and was out the front door before either of his parents had time to answer.

As soon as he could, he cut off the quiet streets of DeVere Heights and scrambled down to the beach. He ran at the edge of the shore. Ran until his lungs were burning and his legs were aching. And then he kept on running. He welcomed the pain in his body. If it kept him from thinking, he'd keep running.

But half an hour later, he had to stop. He dropped onto the cool sand, his chest heaving as he gasped for breath.

Slowly, as he stared up at the huge arc of sky above him, his breathing returned to normal and he realized the exertion had cleared his head. There was no way he could deal with his life without Sienna in it. But there was obviously no way they could continue their relationship in the face of all the parental negativity.

He knew what he and Sienna had to do.

And tomorrow, he'd tell her.

"No, turn a little more to the left," Adam told Belle at the cafeteria table the next day. "A little more . . . stop. Perfect."

"This is a little extreme, don't you think?" Belle laughed.

"Not at all, and keep still!" Adam instructed.

Belle sat absolutely still for all of about two seconds

before collapsing into giggles again. Adam shook his head in despair and adjusted himself so that his body blocked Jason's face from the door. "When you've stopped laughing," he said, frowning at Belle, "you're blocking Sienna, and I'm blocking Jason. There will be no lip-reading on our watch."

"You're too funny!" Belle exclaimed, settling into position. "Nobody is here to lip-read, anyway. We're *inside*. No one sits inside for lunch. I didn't even know there was an inside until today."

"Joke all you want," Adam replied. "Just don't move." He shot a sideways glance at Jason. "Okay. You're clear."

"Good. Now tell me what's going on," Sienna said. She started to lean toward Jason, but Adam *tsk-tsk*ed her back into place.

Jason swallowed hard, gazing at her gorgeous face. Adam and Belle could have been on another planet, as far as he was concerned. They were there for camouflage, nothing else.

"I know what we have to do," Jason said. He took a deep breath. "I think we have to . . . We have to go back . . ."

". . . to being just friends," Sienna finished for him. "I know. I was up all night thinking about it. I won't be able to take it if I get sent away from you. At least this way, we can still see each other."

"And talk to each other," Jason said. *Just not ever touch each other,* he added silently.

"It's going to be so hard," Sienna breathed.

"It's going to be killer," Jason agreed. "But we can do it. We *have* to do it. And you know that we can. We did it for most of last semester."

Sienna gave a faint smile. "We did. And it won't be forever. My parents aren't going to have control of me for my whole life or anything. At college, things will be different. I just wish . . ." She glanced over at Belle and Adam, who were doing a good job of pretending that they were deep in conversation themselves, trying to give Sienna and Jason at least the illusion of being alone.

"You just wish what?" Jason prompted.

"I just wish that the last time we kissed, I'd known it was the last time," she told him.

"The last time for a while," he corrected. But he felt exactly the same way.

"Right, the last time *for a while*," Sienna agreed. "I just would have tried to lock the memory away. So I could keep it safe."

All Jason wanted to do right at that moment was kiss her. Give her that memory. Give them both that memory.

But it was too risky.

One kiss, and he could lose her completely.

EIGHT

"Look, I know why you're so upset," Adam said to Jason as they waited for chemistry class to start.

"Really? Because I didn't realize you were sitting a foot away from me when Sienna and I broke up," Jason said, the words slippery with sarcasm.

"Not that. Why you're *really* upset," Adam went on, mock-serious. "You're afraid you're going to flunk out of French without Sienna to help you. And I want you to know that you don't have to worry, because I'm taking over as your tutor."

"Adam, you can't even *say* the word 'croissant'. Forget about spelling it," Jason reminded him.

"Untrue. Okay, it's sort of true," Adam admitted. "I prefer the American term 'crescent roll.' But I can recite most of the lines from *Amélie* flawlessly. I even sound like Audrey Tautou, who played Amélie, which I'm sure you know, since you never miss a film directed by the genius Jean-Pierre Jeunet."

Jason laughed. He hadn't expected that. He hadn't expected to laugh again, well, pretty much ever. "Okay, you're on. You're my new French tutor," he told Adam.

Adam rattled off a whole bunch of what might

have been French, though it didn't sound like anything Madame Goddard had ever uttered.

"I have no idea what you just said," Jason admitted.

"'Amélie has one friend, Blubber. Alas, the home environment has made Blubber suicidal,'" Adam translated. "'It happens right at this point where a goldfish jumps out of the bowl, trying to commit suicide. So fun—'"

"Why don't I think any of that is going to be on Goddard's midterm?" Jason interrupted.

"Don't worry, I know other stuff. Meet me in the parking lot after school and we'll get started," Adam replied.

"Cool," Jason said. But he felt a dull ache roll through his body as he realized he'd never have another French lesson with Sienna. This just-friends thing—it was going to be even harder than he'd thought.

Jason leaned against the Bug, watching Sienna and Belle head across the school parking lot. He knew it would be better not to even look at her. Or easier at least. But looking was pretty much all he had right now, so he was going to look.

Although, maybe he could do a little bit more than look. Sienna was with Belle, after all, so if he went over, he wouldn't be alone with Sienna. And that's what Sienna's parents had forbidden: he and Sienna being alone together.

But Jason had only taken two steps toward her when Brad stepped up beside him, looped one arm over Jason's shoulders, and turned him back toward his car. *What's this about?* Jason thought. *Christ! Is Adam right about Brad?* "What's up?" Jason asked.

"You don't want to go over there right now," Brad said softly. "Sienna's car broke down again, and her dad's come to pick her up. Check it out. At four o'clock."

Jason shot a quick glance in that direction. Mr. Devereux sat behind the wheel of a nearby Bentley. "Thanks," Jason told Brad.

"Not a problem," Brad answered. "I know you and Sienna are getting a lot of flack from her parents."

Man, I've got paranoid, Jason thought. *Brad's my friend. He's Sienna's friend. He just proved that. And he shouldn't have needed to prove anything!*

"Study time!" came a voice from behind him.

Jason turned to face the voice and saw Adam heading toward him, with Michael Van Dyke, Aaron Harberts, and Kyle Priesmeyer from the swim team.

Adam jumped in the shotgun seat of the Bug. Harberts and Priesmeyer took the backseat. And Brad and Van Dyke piled into Brad's Jeep. "Well, get in," Adam called to Jason. "This heap isn't going to drive itself to Venice."

"How does going to Venice help me pass French?" Jason asked as he climbed into the driver's seat.

"It doesn't," Harberts told him. "But it does help you pass Fun, which, from the looks of you, is a subject you also need help in."

Jason got it. The grapevine really did work fast. They all knew what he was going through with Sienna. Harberts and Priesmeyer probably didn't have the whole story, but they still knew something had gone down and that Jason wasn't happy about it. And this trip was their way of showing support.

"Drive," Priesmeyer ordered. "Brad and Van Dyke are already pulling out of the parking lot."

Jason drove. "So where exactly in Venice do you want to go?" he asked as they flew down PCH.

"Is there more than one destination?" Harberts asked. "The boardwalk."

"I actually haven't been there yet," Jason admitted.

"You really do need help," Harberts said. "There are more hot girls on Rollerblades at the Venice boardwalk than anyplace else in the entire world. And they usually wear very little clothing."

Jason didn't care about that. Not unless one of the girls happened to be Sienna Devereux, but he kept his mouth shut. You didn't tell a car full of guys that the only babe you wanted to see was your girlfriend. Your ex-girlfriend. Your very platonic, only-speak-in-public friend.

"This is the exit," Priesmeyer announced. "Go left. Ocean turns into Pacific, and that slams right into the boardwalk."

Jason followed Priesmeyer's instructions and pulled into a medium-size parking lot near one end of the boardwalk. He took the spot next to Brad's Jeep.

"I've got to eat," Van Dyke said. "We're hitting Sausage Kingdom first. No argument."

"You're not getting one from me. My dad actually sent me to school with leftover ten-alarm chili today," Adam answered. "I'm running on empty."

Van Dyke took the lead, weaving through the crowd on the boardwalk, which was really just a sidewalk running right along the beach. Jason tried not to stare at the insanity that bombarded them from all sides. He tried to remind himself that he was a native now. But, good God, that guy had an albino boa constrictor wrapped around his neck! The thing was so big, its tail almost touched the ground. And it definitely wasn't stuffed because its slick black tongue kept flicking out of its mouth, tasting the air. Who did that? Who walked around wearing a killer reptile as a necktie?

"I can't believe the grain of rice stand is still open," Brad said, gesturing to a little sidewalk stand. "Why would anyone want to get their name written on a grain of rice in the first place?"

"Look, it's the roller-skating, guitar-playing dude," Priesmeyer said. "You can't make your first trip to the boardwalk without seeing him," he told Jason. "The guy's a local legend."

"A legendary freak," Van Dyke put in, watching the guy in the flowing robe skate past, strumming away.

"Van Dyke used to be afraid of him," Brad explained. "He literally wet his pants the first time he saw the guy."

"I was four," Van Dyke said. "And I grew up in the Heights. I'd never seen anything like him. I thought he was an evil wizard."

"Oooh. My favorite henna tattoo chick is working the booth today. I've been fantasizing about how it would feel to have her do one of those Hindu designs on my head. I'm all fresh shaved." Priesmeyer ran his hands over his gleaming scalp. "Today is the day to make my fantasy come true. I'll catch up with you." He veered off toward the brightly colored tattoo tent.

Jason and the other four guys kept walking. They paused for a few minutes by an outdoor weightlifting area. "Muscle Beach," Harberts explained. "This is Brad's fantasy. Watching oiled-up musclemen in Speedos."

Brad slapped him on the back of the head. "We stopped for you, Harberts."

Harberts gave a snort and moved on down the boardwalk. Jason and the others fell in beside him.

"Well, here's my fantasy," Van Dyke said. He jerked his chin toward Sausage Kingdom. "Jody Maroni's sausages. And lots of them." He sat down at one of the empty tables outside the food stand.

"Eating some sausage and watching the Rollergirls. Not bad for a Wednesday afternoon," Harberts said.

"Not for you, Harberts. You should stick to a wheatgrass smoothie or something," Brad joked. "Your time in the medley has been for crap. You don't need any extra weight dragging you down. In fact, I've been meaning to suggest you start shaving your head like Priesmeyer to get a little less drag in the water."

"I was thinking of suggesting you shave your legs," Van Dyke added. "Me, I think I should pack on a few pounds. Just to make the competition interesting. It's so dull when I have the best time meet after meet without really trying."

He handed Harberts a fifty. "I want an apple maple, a sweet Italian, and an orange-garlic-cumin."

"Why am I waiting in line for you?" Harberts complained.

"Because I'm holding the table. And I can swim your ass off," Van Dyke said. "And while you're at it, get an assortment of the finest for my friend Freeman here. My treat. The rest of you bozos are on your own, though."

Jason grinned, appreciating the gesture from Van Dyke. Not that it helped get his mind off Sienna. All the sausages on the planet wouldn't help *that*. His name engraved on a grain of rice wouldn't help. A couple of dozen supermodels on skates wouldn't help. It was an impossible task. But still, it was good to know that his friends were there for moral support.

"Thanks for arranging this," Jason told Adam. "But you know you're actually going to have to help me with French at some point, right?" he continued. "Because I will seriously not pass if somebody doesn't help me."

"After school tomorrow. My place," Adam promised. "French will be conjugated and otherwise humiliated. It'll be good for me, too. Get me ready for the ladies. You know how they all go crazy for French, the language of *lurve* and all."

"Please open your French textbook to page 103," Adam instructed the next afternoon. He and Jason sat in the Turnball kitchen, a jumbo bag of sea salt and vinegar chips open in front of them and a couple of Mountain Dews to wash them down.

Jason obediently opened his book and saw the little story about Jacques and Pauline at the Tour de France. "Crap!" he exclaimed. "Everything makes me think of Sienna. Even page 103 of my French book."

"How'd it go today—with the friend thing?" Adam asked.

"She and Belle went someplace off-campus for lunch." Jason said. "So I only really saw her in European history. Cauldwell has us doing these group projects, and I'm not in her group, so . . ."

"Got it," Adam said.

"It's probably better that way. Easier," Jason added.

Adam nodded, but it didn't look like Jason had convinced him. Which made sense. Jason hadn't actually convinced himself.

"Okay, I've decided that we're going to use the same method to study French as I did when I taught myself Klingon in the fourth grade," Adam explained.

"Oh, my God. You have just revealed a whole new level of nerdiness," Jason told his friend.

"I had to learn it to do the voices for the documentary I made with my action figures," Adam explained.

"I don't think you can make a documentary with dolls," Jason said.

"*Action figures*. And I was ahead of my time," Adam answered. "Someday that documentary is going to be recognized as the beginning of Adam Turnball's brilliant directing career."

"How does this have anything to do with French again?" Jason asked.

"Me learning Klingon. Which is a much more

difficult language than French," Adam said. "What I basically did was take part in this Klingon Language Institute project to translate the Bible—Old and New Testaments—into Klingon."

"Uh, I think the Bible has already been translated into French," Jason commented.

"That would be a little beyond the two of us anyway. Although Madame Goddard would probably shell out some bonus points if we gave it a shot," Adam answered. "The thing is, during the project, I e-mailed a lot of people—in Klingon—and that got me pretty proficient." He stood up. "So come on."

"Come on where?" Jason asked.

"To the computer. I found a chat room where everybody writes in French. We're going to hang in there, improve our skills, get some pointers," Adam explained.

Jason snagged his soda and the chips. "Worth a try. Doing some writing and translating can't hurt my French grade."

"Oh, we're definitely going to get you at least a C on the midterm," Adam promised. "Plus, we might hook up with some *très jolie* French babes."

Très jolie. The words sent Jason back to lying on Sienna's bed with her, "studying" French.

"Damn, I got you thinking about her again, didn't I?" Adam asked as they headed toward his room.

"Doesn't matter. Everything does it." Jason hoisted his Mountain Dew. "Even this. I was drinking one of these when I talked to Sienna at my first DeVere Heights party. The one at Brad's. She accused me of bogarting the Dew."

"So are you going to the party at Ryan's? If you want to avoid it—and the hours of Sienna-proximity torture—the two of us could do something else," Adam offered.

"No, I want to go. I can't wait actually," Jason said with a lopsided grin. "All those hours of Sienna-proximity torture."

NINE

"I can't believe Mom and Dad gave me permission to go to Ryan's party," Dani said sarcastically to Jason as they walked down their driveway. "His place is two whole houses away from ours! I might, I don't know, get lost on the way home."

Or you might, I don't know, fall in love with a vampire, Jason thought. *And end up like me.*

"Wow. Look at the Patricks' yard," Dani breathed. Glass hearts—some red, some white—hung from the branches of every tree, glowing with the light of the candles that burned inside. More candles—these as long and thick as Dani's arm—had been staked into the ground on both sides of the walkway leading to the front door. And somehow, Jason couldn't quite figure out the mechanics of how, a second moon was suspended over the house, full and silvery, looking almost as real as the one nature made.

"It's so romantic," Dani said as they cut across the street.

Jason was suddenly struck by the fact that this was a Valentine's party. It was all going to be about couples. He was probably the only guy there without a date. Well, except Adam. Adam didn't do the dating thing much. He claimed he had a rare disease that made him sound like an idiot whenever he was around a girl he liked.

"No offense, but I don't want to walk in with my brother," Dani said. "I'll see you in there." She picked up her pace and, a few moments later, disappeared through the open double doors leading inside.

Jason wasn't ready to go in anyway. He was beginning to feel like this was a big mistake. He spotted a stone bench under one of the trees and headed over. He decided he'd sit there for a while, and then, if he still felt like the party was going to be a torture fest, he'd take off and swing by for Dani later.

He leaned back against the trunk of the tree and watched people drift into the party. Lots of couples, just like he'd thought. *Sienna wouldn't show with someone else, would she?* he wondered suddenly. *We're not trying that hard to fool her parents. Are we?*

No, there she was. Walking slowly through the candlelight. Her hair pulled up, showing off her long neck. God, she was gorgeous. She hadn't seen him, and he didn't call out to her.

"Why didn't I bring my camera?"

Jason smiled, recognizing Adam's voice.

"I could use a few more shots of sad and lonely boy by candlelight," Adam continued, stopping next to the bench.

"And you aren't sad and lonely?" Jason asked with a grin. He looked up at the glimmering glass hearts above their heads. "And also by candlelight. Or is there a girl with you I don't see?"

"Belle is meeting me here," Adam answered.

Wait. Adam and Belle? Wasn't Adam the one who'd spelled out the reasons why a vampire-human combo wasn't all that great? "*Belle's* meeting you here?" Jason repeated, trying to wrap his head around the fact.

"Not like that," Adam told him. "Belle has decided I'm much too groovy to be single. She's making it her mission to find me the perfect girl sometime tonight, at this very party. Her one condition was that I didn't bring the camera along."

"In that case, I'd like to add a condition too," Jason said.

Adam raised his eyebrows.

"Don't mention the Klingon Language Institute until you're . . . until you're married. Maybe have a couple of kids," Jason told him.

Adam shook his head. "Ass. So are you going in? Or are you continuing to brood—or whatever it is you're doing?"

"I'm sticking with the whatever for a while. Sienna's in there. I thought it would be great just to see her. But I'm not sure I can take it."

"I feel you," Adam said. He started to sit down on the bench.

"No way. Get in there. If Belle can't hook you up, no one can," Jason told him.

Adam grinned. "I know. I have the best wingman—wingchick?—going. I cannot help but score."

"As long as you speak English only," Jason reminded him.

Adam shouted something guttural and unintelligible as he started for the house. "That's 'screw you' in Klingon," he called over his shoulder.

So much for hanging with Adam tonight, Jason thought. But he probably shouldn't really do the lonely guy by candlelight thing either. That was just too pathetic. He shoved himself to his feet and walked straight into the party.

Wild! he thought as he looked around. Somehow Jason didn't think Ryan's mom had helped with the decorations—at least not inside. There was another one of those freaky how-do-they-do-that? moons beaming down from the ceiling, and there were go-go girls—that was the only way to describe them—all over the place, shimmying to the music. They wore shiny white vinyl thigh-high boots and shiny white vinyl cupid wings. A few pieces of lacy red material—and a few strategic heart tattoos—completed their outfits.

"How much do I love Ryan Patrick right now?" Van Dyke asked from behind Jason. He held a plate with some lobster, some cinnamon hearts, and some strawberries on it. "He's got to have collected all the red food in the state—and hired every unemployed model in Hollywood," he added with a grin.

"Seems that way," Jason agreed, smiling back.

"Uh-oh. Here comes my date. She'll be pissed if she catches me looking," Van Dyke said. He put his plate down, rushed across the room, and swept Maggie into a deep dip straight out of a chick flick. He kissed her as the go-go cupids boogied around them.

Jason didn't need to be watching this. A drink is what he *did* need. Make that drinks. *Lots* of drinks. He wasn't driving, so no worries on that front. He spotted a goofy fountain of deep red punch on a table to one side of the room. He was sure it would be spiked, but syrupy sweet drinks weren't good for the long haul.

He decided to check out the kitchen for beer. Sure enough, Jason spotted a trashcan full of iced beers as soon as he stepped into the room. But a half a second later, he spotted Sienna. She was sitting on the counter, laughing at some story Lauren Gissinger was telling.

Jason backed out of the room quickly. He knew it was

totally within the just-friends rules to walk over and join the group. But he also knew there was no way he could get that close to Sienna and not want to touch her. And that was too risky. "Punch it is," he muttered.

He strode back out to the fountain, dipped himself a cupful of the red stuff, and downed it. It was definitely spiked. He quickly refilled his cup, then decided to check out the backyard. Who knew what Ryan had going on poolside?

The first thing he saw was Erin Henry feeding on Harberts in the hot tub. Red and pink rose petals swirled around them, matching the dinner plate–size blossoms in the huge vases all around the pool. To non-vampires it would look like the couple were just making out, but Jason knew better. He also knew exactly how radical Harberts was feeling right now. When the vampires drank from you it was like getting a bliss injection. Like getting high on the best drug ever created.

Jason turned away, not wanting to think about anything vampiric. He heard the rhythmic thump of a dribbling basketball and quickly found the source. A lighted outdoor court. Full size. Now *that* he could handle. Jason chugged his punch, grabbed a beer out of the ice-filled garbage can near the diving board, and made his way over to the court.

Brad and Priesmeyer were playing one-on-one. As Jason approached, Brad made a perfect basket from half-court. "And that's it. Priesmeyer goes down!" he cheered. A couple of girls applauded from the sidelines. "Who's next?"

"Me," Jason called.

Brad threw him the ball, and they were on. Jason pounded down the court—but Brad got in front of him, blocking him.

Brad's superstrength and supernatural speed made him a killer opponent. But basketball wasn't all about the physical. Jason feinted left. Brad fell for it, and Jason managed to duck around him and . . . "He shoots, he scores!" Jason cried.

But then Brad shot, and scored—twice. Jason pulled off his sweater and tossed it off the court. Time to get serious.

Even at absolute seriousness, Brad won 11 to 9. But since Jason wasn't supernatural, he felt pretty good about those nine points.

"Good game," Brad said.

"Thanks." Jason used the hem of his T-shirt to wipe the sweat off his face. "I definitely need another beer after that." He snatched up his sweater.

"I'm buying," Brad joked as he led the way back to the garbage can stuffed with beers.

Jason stared at the fake moon above the Patrick house. "Does one of Ryan's parents work at a movie studio or something? That's one hell of a special effect."

"No. His dad's a lawyer. And his mom is a VP at the DeVere Center for Advanced Genetics and Blood Research."

So that made it absolutely clear: Ryan and his family were vampires. There was no way you could get to be a VP at that place with blunt teeth. Sienna's dad was on the board there. Maybe a few non-vampires held some lower-level positions, but quite possibly not even that.

"I don't know Ryan very well," Jason said, doing a little fishing. "It was cool of him to invite me to the party."

"That's Ryan. He'd invite everybody in Malibu if they'd fit in the house," Brad said with a grin. "Belle has this whole system of classifying guys by what kind of dog they'd be if they were dogs, and she says Ryan's a golden retriever: likes everyone, everyone likes him."

I guess if Dani has to date a vampire, it's good that he's also a golden retriever, Jason thought wryly.

"I'm heading back inside. I want to dance with a go-go girl. Those wings—they make me nuts," Brad said. "And I *am* a single guy again. You coming?"

"In a while," Jason answered. He wasn't ready to paste a smile on his face and dive back into the crowd. He headed down to the beach, scrambling down the cliffside to the sand.

It was deserted, which was unusual for a DeVere

Heights party. Generally the beach was the main event. But it was chilly out tonight, and Ryan's house didn't have stairs down to the sand. It was probably just as well that people weren't clambering down the cliff drunk. Jason took a breath of crisp nighttime air and walked down to the sea. A little way farther along the shore a few boulders were scattered at the waterline, the black ocean lapping gently at their bases.

The real moon sailed high in the sky, casting a silver glow over the sand and turning the water to shiny obsidian. Jason had never seen the Pacific so calm before. He walked for a while, making for the boulders. It was nice to be away from the noise and the heat of the party.

He skirted the boulders. And, suddenly, there she was. Waist-deep in the water, the moon glinting softly off her dark hair: Sienna.

She trailed one pale hand through the still ocean, dragging ripples of silver in her wake.

Jason stood still, afraid to move. Afraid to breathe. Afraid to ruin the perfection that was Sienna at that moment.

Then she turned toward him, as if she felt his eyes on her. She started to smile as she took a step closer to shore. Then she froze. He could tell she was remembering the new rules too.

Just friends, a voice whispered in his head. *Friends.*

But the adrenaline coursing through his veins told a different story.

They just stood there. Both staring. Then Sienna moved forward, just a tiny bit, a small step toward Jason.

That's all it took. Jason was moving toward her, running into the ocean. She held out her arms as he reached her, and he pulled her up against him. Her mouth was on his, hot and wet and perfect.

Some small part of Jason's brain was still telling him this shouldn't be happening. That he should stop it. But that was an impossibility. Take his hands off her warm skin? Take his mouth away from her lips? Complete impossibility.

He didn't care what happened. All that mattered was now: this minute, this night. He and Sienna alone on the beach together.

TEN

"I'm sorry." Sienna backed away from Jason, fingers pressed to her lips.

"Don't," he told her. "Don't say you're sorry. Not for that."

Sienna smiled. "You're right. We don't have anything to apologize for. You go to a party, you have some drinks, you end up kissing one of your friends, right?"

"Right," Jason said. "This pretty much falls into the friend category. That punch Ryan's dishing out is lethal. I'm surprised I didn't end up kissing Adam."

Sienna laughed. A completely fake laugh.

"Although I guess I'd have had to wait in line. Belle has made it her mission to find Adam his dream girl," Jason added. *Why am I talking about Adam when I'm finally alone with Sienna?* he thought.

"It's good for her," Sienna answered. "It keeps her mind off Dom." She looked down at the ground, like she was fascinated by the sand at her feet.

"So, we're good, right?" Jason asked, because it didn't feel exactly like they were.

"We're good. We're friends. Everything is . . . it's

okay," Sienna murmured, eyes still on the ground.

He wasn't finding it easy looking at her, either. Not standing so close. Not when he could still feel that kiss.

"Do you think anyone saw?" Jason asked.

Sienna glanced nervously up and down the beach. "I doubt it. There's no cover anywhere. If anyone else was out here, we'd see them, right?"

"Right," Jason said. "We're alone."

They stared at each other for a moment.

"I need to go home," Sienna said in a rush. "I'm going to take the beach route. I'll . . . I'll see you at school, Jason." She turned around and hurried away from him.

"Wait!" Jason called.

Sienna looked over her shoulder.

"Let me walk you," he offered.

Sienna just stared at him.

"Except how stupid would that be? Me walking you to your house—where your parents live," Jason continued.

"Pretty stupid," Sienna said softly. She started away again, her arms wrapped tightly around her body.

"Wait!" Jason called again. He couldn't stop himself. "At least take my sweater. You look like you're freezing." He didn't even know if vampires felt the cold the way humans did, but she looked cold, the way she was rubbing her arms with her hands. Maybe she was just feeling uncomfortable, already regretting what they'd done.

"Here." Jason tossed her the sweater. He didn't trust himself to get close enough to hand it to her. Not without kissing her again.

Sienna wrapped the sweater around her shoulders. "It smells like you," she told him. "And you always look after me—make me feel safe," she added dreamily, almost as if she were talking to herself. "I love that."

Jason smiled. He didn't know what to say.

Sienna shook herself out of the daydream. "It's late," she said. "I'll see you at school."

At school. In a group of people. Where they would never be alone together again.

I'm not doing lonely guy standing on the beach, Jason told himself as he watched Sienna hurry away. He turned and climbed up the cliff, got himself another beer, and reentered party central. Which had turned into make-out central while he'd been gone. It seemed like every available space was taken up by groping couples. He couldn't take it. He was out of there. But first he needed to tell Dani.

He did a pass through the first floor. Didn't see her. Although he definitely noticed Adam. His friend was holding court on the big leather couch, surrounded by about six girls, all of them giggling at something he'd said. Belle sat next to him, grinning.

Jason left him to it and headed upstairs. The first door he opened was a screening room. Of course. What Malibu mansion was complete without one? The credits of what looked like the *Snakes on a Plane* sequel were rolling. A moment later, the lights came up.

"Jason, you missed a great movie!" Dani exclaimed when she spotted him.

It seemed like Dani had missed a great movie too—considering that about half of her lipstick had ended up on Ryan Patrick's mouth.

"I'm heading home," Jason told her. "Are you coming?"

"I guess so," Dani answered. "Ryan's parents are going to be home soon, anyway. They don't want things to run too late."

"Thanks for the invite," Jason said to Ryan.

"Anytime," Ryan answered with a grin. "Don't forget to grab your gift bags. They're laid out in the front hall." He reached over and kissed Dani lightly on the lips. "Good night," he said softly, and Dani smiled.

I guess he definitely is her don't-want-to-talk-about-it-guy, Jason thought. *Well, at least Brad seems to think he's decent. Hell, he even looks like a golden retriever with all that blond hair and the big brown eyes.*

Jason half-turned to give them some privacy while

they said their good-byes. Then Dani joined him.
They grabbed their gift bags and headed home.

"Ooooh. Bumble and bumble products. I love
Bumble and bumble," Dani cooed, peering into the
bag. "And the new Killers CD. It's not supposed to
drop for a month and a half. How extreme is that? A
toe ring. I guess that's why they divided the bags into
girls and guys."

Jason tuned his sister out. He couldn't stop thinking about Dani and Ryan. It was kind of strange that
they hadn't even tried to hide the fact that they'd been
making out. *Then again,* he thought, *most of the other
vampires don't hide their make-out sessions either.* And
with that, a sickening thought sliced into Jason's head.
Has Ryan been drinking my sister's blood?

Jason staggered downstairs around noon the next
morning. Head pounding, eyes blurry, stomach churn-
ing. He knew he shouldn't have mixed that punch with
. . . well, he shouldn't have drunk that punch, period.

"You're up early," Dani teased. She had all kinds
of crap for what seemed like a diorama laid out in
front of her on the coffee table. *Happy Days* blared
from the TV.

"Does that have to be so loud?" Jason asked.

Dani took the volume down a few levels. "Better?"

Jason grunted as he sank down on the couch. "What

are you doing, anyway?" He nodded toward her project.

"Designing a set for one of the scenes in *A Midsummer Night's Dream*. English assignment," she answered.

"You're doing homework? Now?" Just speaking and breathing was all Jason could handle after the party. "Didn't you get dented last night?"

"Nope. Having too much fun with Ryan," Dani replied.

Jason squinted at her, trying to figure out if she'd been fed on or not. If she had, she should still be feeling happy, but not the cheerful, energetic happy she was demonstrating, woozy happy, what-did-I-do-last-night? happy.

"What movie were you guys watching last night, anyway?" Jason asked, to test her memory.

"Some straight-to-DVD spoof of *Snakes on a Plane*," Dani said. "It's so stupid. That movie was practically a spoof to begin with."

So, memory—okay.

Jason watched as Dani carefully glued a tree to the bottom of a cardboard box. Manual dexterity—okay.

"My head feels like a balloon full of whipped cream and rocks," Jason told her. "You're sure you're feeling all right?" Dani looked up at him and smiled. "Jason, if you want to know if Ryan drank my blood last night, just ask."

ELEVEN

"What?" Jason spluttered.

"Ryan didn't feed from me," Dani said calmly. "He would never do that."

Jason gazed at his sister in astonishment.

She stared right back at him. "You might want to close your mouth," she suggested. "You look like a goldfish."

"I can't believe you!" Jason finally burst out. "You *know*? You know about the—"

"Vampires?" Dani finished for him. "Well, I do now. Although I hear *you've* known for ages." She crossed her arms over her chest and raised an eyebrow. "Thanks for clueing me in."

Jason shook his head and gave a little laugh, still reeling. "Sorry."

"Why didn't you tell me?"

"It was a secret," Jason explained. "And it wasn't my secret to tell."

"But you told Adam, right?" Dani demanded. "Ryan says Adam knows all about them."

"Actually, Adam told me," Jason explained. "He'd already done tons of vampire research before I even met him."

"So all this time you knew what was going on and I didn't." Dani took a seat next to him on the sofa, abandoning her project. "No wonder you never backed me up about all the parties Mom and Dad wouldn't let me go to."

"I was afraid somebody would feed on you," Jason admitted. "It happened once, you know, before I knew about the vampires."

Dani's expression grew clouded. "Yeah, I thought so. I mean, not at the time, but once Ryan told me how it all works. I looked back and realized . . ."

"Me too." Jason thought about Erin Henry and how she'd once fed on him at a party. "It's not the worst feeling in the world."

"True," Dani agreed with a grin.

"But afterward, when you know what really went on, it's a little weird."

Dani nodded. "Do you and Sienna . . . ? Do you let her drink your blood?" Dani asked.

"No. Well, I did once," Jason told her. "But only because she needed it. She was dying."

"Wow! Romantic!" Dani exclaimed.

Jason studied her face. She obviously thought the whole dating-a-vampire thing *was* pretty romantic. "I don't know if I'd call it that," Jason said carefully. "I had no choice, and neither did Sienna. It was more about sur- vival than romance. Just hanging out, kissing, holding hands, all the usual stuff—that's romantic. The vampire part is mostly just a complication."

"I guess," Dani said thoughtfully. "But it's also pretty cool, you have to admit. Did you know they can change the way they look? Ryan showed me his real appearance—and he's even more gorgeous than he looks normally!"

"Yeah, I—"

"Plus, he's incredibly strong," Dani went on. "And fast. It's like they're humans, but they're just sort of *better* at it than everyone else."

"I wouldn't put it that way," Jason said. "They're not better, they're just different." He didn't really want his sister getting some kind of starry-eyed idea about the vampires. Dating one of them wasn't the kind of situation she should walk into without some serious consideration.

"Listen, Dani," he said seriously. "I know it probably feels like a TV show or something, dating a wealthy, good-looking vampire, but—"

"A wealthy, good-looking, incredibly *sweet* vampire," Dani cut in.

"Still, this isn't a television series," Jason insisted. "It seems like you're only paying attention to the vampire traits you like. But you can't ignore the fact that there are bad things, too. It's dangerous to date a vampire. It can be life and death."

"You mean the crossbow killer," Dani said. "Ryan

told me that guy who shot you was really a vampire hunter. He said you figured it out—which is incredibly studly of you, by the way."

"Thanks. I think," Jason said dubiously. "But that's not what I meant. Do you want to know how I originally found out about the vampires? Turns out there was a renegade vampire in town. A vampire who was giving in to his bloodlust. Did Ryan even tell you about bloodlust?"

Dani chewed on her lip. "Nooo . . ."

"It's what happens if a vampire lets their hunger get out of control. The need for blood consumes them and they keep on drinking, even if it kills the human. That's what really happened to Carrie Smith the night of Belle's party."

Dani's eyes widened. "Are you serious?"

"Yes."

"Wow." Dani looked thoughtful. "I can't imagine Ryan ever being like that. Or Sienna."

"No, it doesn't happen often," Jason admitted. "And the vampires dealt with it pretty quickly. But I saw the guy's eyes when I fought him—he was off the hook. And vampires are outrageously strong, so if one wants to kill you, well, you're dead."

"Why are you talking like this?" Dani asked. "You're in love with a vampire. You're friends with vampires. You like them."

"That's true." Jason ran a hand through his hair. "I don't know. I just don't want you to get hurt."

"Are you getting hurt?"

"Hell, yeah," Jason said with a rueful laugh. "Emotionally, anyway. Sienna's parents won't let us see each other. And that hurts like you wouldn't believe." Jason took his sister's hand. "Look, I just don't want you to end up feeling like I've been feeling lately. It's not fun. So just . . . don't get in over your head. You've only known Ryan for a few weeks."

"But that's enough," Dani told him. "I know everything about him. I know he loves me. And I know I'm safe with him."

"Okay," Jason said. "Then I'm happy for you."

But as his sister headed upstairs to her room, Jason felt a stab of worry. He had a feeling Dani didn't know as much as she thought she did. Had Ryan really made it clear to her what a big deal it was to have a vampire-human romance? And what about Ryan's parents? Why hadn't they reacted the same way that Sienna's had?

Suddenly Jason realized the truth: Ryan's parents didn't know about the relationship! Dani and Ryan had been keeping it low-key, at least up until the party last night. But now that Dani and Ryan were out of the closet, the Patricks would be sure to find out soon.

And then they would forbid Ryan to see Danielle.

Jason sighed. He didn't want Dani to go through what he was going through. But he had to admit it: He'd be relieved when she and Ryan broke up.

"'Describe in one sentence the theme of William Faulkner's *The Sound and the Fury*,'" Jason read aloud from his English notebook. "Great," he said to himself. "I haven't even finished reading that book."

He let his pen drop onto the notebook, sat back in the deck chair, and stretched. He'd been planning to do his homework out by the pool, but the combination of late afternoon sunshine, birdsong, and the after-effects of last night's party had made him sleepy. And it didn't help that now he was alone in the house. His parents had gone out with Mr. Freeman's boss, to some famous restaurant in Beverly Hills.

Dani was out too, with Ryan. She'd been wearing a huge, dreamy smile when she left. Jason felt a little guilty for wanting her relationship to end. After all, he knew just how it felt to be besotted with a vampire. It was exciting and unexpected and more than a little addictive. He knew he shouldn't have one set of rules for himself and another for Dani. But she was his baby sister. He couldn't help feeling protective.

Besides, she barely knew Ryan. She couldn't really be in love with him already. It was a totally different situation from his own with Sienna. He'd known

Sienna for months, and they'd fought their attraction like crazy before they finally—

Yeah, right, Jason thought. *We fought our attraction because Sienna was going out with Brad. It had nothing to do with the vampire thing. I'd have been with her from day one if she'd crooked her finger. And finding out she was a vampire wouldn't have changed that.*

Jason lurched to his feet, pulled off his shirt, and dove into the pool, letting the chilly water shock him out of his thoughts about Sienna. He couldn't let himself go there, because thinking about Sienna would lead to thinking about last night's events. And just the memory of Sienna's body pressed against his was enough to make him lose his mind.

After a couple of laps he climbed out and headed over to the pool house for a towel. He dried off and walked back to the deck chair, surprised to see that the sun had disappeared. A quick glance up showed dark clouds encroaching on the constant blue of the California sky.

The doorbell rang.

Jason jogged through the house to the front door and yanked it open, expecting to see Adam, or maybe just the mailman with a package or something.

He didn't expect Sienna.

"Hey there, Michigan," she said, a smile playing about her mouth. "Did I catch you in the shower?"

"Excuse me?" Jason asked, still trying to process the fact that she was actually standing on his doorstep. He felt alive and awake, all his senses tingling.

"You're dripping." Sienna reached out and playfully tousled his wet hair.

Jason automatically reached for her hand, then stopped himself at the last second. He wasn't supposed to touch her anymore. They were just friends.

Sienna seemed to realize that at the same moment. She snatched her hand away from him. They stared at each other awkwardly for a few seconds.

"I was in the pool," Jason said finally. "Hence the moisture."

"Oh." Sienna nodded. "Well, I should boogie. I'm supposed to be at Belle's, and she can only cover for me for so long before her dad figures it out. I just came by to give this back." She held out the sweater he'd loaned her the night before. "Thank you."

"No problem."

"Okay. So . . . I'll see you later." Sienna turned away, and Jason's heart gave a lurch. He didn't want her to go.

"Wait!" he called.

She turned back immediately. "Yes?"

"Don't you want to come in?" Jason asked.

Sienna raised one eyebrow. "Is coming in a good idea?" she asked.

Jason grabbed her hand—in a friends way, he told

himself. "Oh, just come have a drink. Friends are allowed to do that. And there's no one else home, so no grapevine potential." He tugged her inside, and he couldn't help noticing that she didn't resist too much.

"One drink," she said.

"Right." Jason reluctantly let go of her hand when they reached the kitchen. "What do you want? Coke? Iced tea? I think Dani's got some health water in here somewhere. . . ."

"Do you have any lemonade?" Sienna asked. "I always like to have lemonade out by the pool."

"Lemonade it is." Jason maneuvered things around so that he could get the big pitcher of lemonade from the back of the refrigerator.

"I'll grab glasses." Sienna immediately pulled open the right cabinet and took out two tall glasses. Jason watched her, remembering when she was allowed to just come hang out at his house because she was his girl-friend. Now even something as simple as having a drink seemed illicit somehow. "Any sparks between Adam and the girls Belle found for him?" Sienna asked.

"I'm not sure. I don't think Adam got to have a say in it." Jason laughed. "I think Belle was planning to decide for him whether there were sparks or not."

"She's got good taste. I wonder if she already has a dinner date set up," Sienna replied. "She'll probably tag along and coach him on what to say, too."

Jason poured the lemonade and led the way out to the pool. "I don't know how nice it will be today. It looks like rain." He peered up at the clouds.

Sienna stood next to him and glanced at the sky. "It never rains in California," she informed him.

A huge wet *splat!* on Jason's arm made him laugh. "Is that so?" he asked.

Sienna grinned. "Yes. It doesn't rain. It pours. Like you wouldn't believe."

Another drop hit his shoulder. Then another.

Sienna was already running for the pool house. "Hesitate and suffer!" she called.

Jason looked up—just as the skies opened. Rain poured down on him as if he were standing under a waterfall. "Gaaahhh!" he cried, sprinting after Sienna.

She was standing just inside the door of the little pool house, laughing. "You baby," she teased. "You were already wet anyway."

"I know, but the water in the pool is heated." Jason shook his head like a dog, spraying water all over Sienna, who squealed and gave him a playful push.

"Welcome to winter in Malibu," Sienna said. "Either it's bright and sunny or it's practically a monsoon."

"I never knew that." Jason reached up and took down one of the extra lounge chairs they kept on a shelf over the pool supplies. He pulled off the dust cover, and he and Sienna sat down together.

"Yup. Winter is rainy season. Sometimes it will rain for two weeks straight. And then there are mudslides."

"That sounds bad," Jason said.

"It is bad. My family did a big charity auction last year for the victims of a mudslide south of here." Sienna sighed, and Jason knew she was thinking of all the charity stuff her parents were making her do lately, just to keep her away from him.

"So all this 'sunny California' stuff is false advertising?" he asked, trying to lighten the mood.

"Hmm. Well, 'sunny California for fifty weeks a year' is not nearly as catchy."

Jason chuckled. They watched the rain pounding the stone patio outside the door. It was a sheet of water, and it made him feel as if they were trapped in their own private little world.

I wish we were, he thought. *Just me and Sienna, alone together. No parents. No rules. Nothing to keep us apart.*

"Why so serious?" Sienna murmured, and Jason realized she'd been staring at him.

"Just thinking. I can't see a thing through the water."

"Me neither." Sienna moved closer, her slender arm brushing against him. "I love the sound of rain. It makes me think of lazy days, just staying inside, lounging around in bed. . . ."

Jason's throat went dry. He knew he should answer her, say something boring and friendlike. But the image of Sienna lounging in bed had driven all other thoughts from his mind. All he could feel was the heat of her body close to his, all he could smell was her perfume, and all he wanted was to press his lips against hers.

"Jason . . ." Sienna turned toward him, and then they were kissing. Her arms slid around his neck, and he clutched her waist and pulled her down on top of him as he lay back on the lounge chair.

The sound of the rain pounded in his ears, keeping time with his galloping heart as he tangled his hands in Sienna's thick hair and deepened their kiss. He felt her fingers slide beneath the waistband of his bathing suit, and his breath caught in his throat. He unzipped her hoodie and eased it down over her shoulders as he kissed his way down her neck and across her collarbone. . . .

We are *alone in our own world,* Jason thought. *No one can see us here. No one will ever know.*

"Should we stop?" he murmured, his mouth on Sienna's throat.

"No," she whispered. "I don't want to stop."

Jason gave himself up to the feel of her lips, her body, her skin, hot and smooth as he slid his hand over her bare stomach.

There was a quiet *click* and the rain seemed louder

suddenly. Jason felt a gust of cold air on his face. He pulled away from Sienna, thinking that the door must have blown free.

"Jason!" Sienna hissed, her eyes wide with fear as she stared at the doorway.

Jason turned his head to see somebody standing there, but it wasn't his parents—or even Dani. It was his aunt Bianca—member of the Vampire High Council—and it was horribly clear that she'd seen everything.

TWELVE

"Aunt Bianca!" Jason cried as he and Sienna scrambled to their feet. Sienna moved as far away as possible in the small pool house, but it was no good. Sienna's hoodie lay in a heap on the floor, and Jason was dressed only in a bathing suit. It was obvious what had been happening.

"Looks like I caught you," Bianca said with a small smile. She was holding an umbrella, but rainwater poured off the edges, landing with little plinking sounds on the tile floor.

Jason sighed. Aunt Bianca had seen them. She knew Sienna's parents. And she was a vampire herself. So even if she wasn't aware of the Devereuxs' ban on their romance, she'd find out soon enough. And she would side with them because she was one of their kind.

"Hello, Sienna," Bianca said. She closed her umbrella and propped it near the door. "I'm assuming your parents don't know where you are."

"I just came to return a sweater I borrowed," Sienna said.

Bianca raised her eyebrows. "Is that what you kids are

calling it nowadays?" Her tone was light and teasing, the way it always was. But Jason thought there was a hint of menace underneath, a menace he'd only caught a glimpse of once before—the day Bianca had decided to execute his friend Tyler for stealing from the vampires.

He hadn't seen Bianca since then. Jason had a feeling he'd never talk to Bianca again without sensing that edge of danger.

"Let's not play games," Bianca went on, briskly. "I know you two aren't supposed to be seeing each other. All I have to do is tell your parents I found you here and they'll send you straight to France, Sienna."

Sienna's dark eyes filled with tears. Jason stood up and reached for her hand. There was no point in pretending now. Sienna's fingers wrapped around his. Jason felt a little better just touching her. "Why would you do that, Aunt Bianca?" he asked. "We love each other. We're not doing anything wrong."

"Love between a vampire and a human is wrong," Bianca replied. "You both know that."

Jason couldn't believe it. She sounded so casual, so normal. But she had basically just admitted that she was aware Jason knew about vampires!

"*You* were a human in love with a vampire once," Sienna pointed out. Her voice shook, and Jason realized she was afraid. As a member of the Vampire High Council, Bianca had a lot of power over Sienna.

"Yes," Bianca acknowledged calmly. "So I think you will agree that I know what I'm talking about. I know how it works. And I know that it *doesn't* work."

"I don't understand," Jason managed. He was still reeling from the shock of Aunt Bianca even being there.

"I *was* a human in love with a vampire," Bianca said. "But I'm not a human now. I haven't been for a long time."

"Right. But you were human when you fell in love with Stefan," Jason said. "And you two made it work. So can we."

"No, you can't. Stefan and I knew we couldn't be together when we were so different," Bianca explained. "So I made a choice. And now I'm giving you the same choice, Jason." Her blue eyes glowed eerily with excitement. "You can do what I did. You can become a vampire."

"What!" Jason exclaimed in shock. Become a vampire? He could barely believe what he was hearing.

"You can transform, like I did." Bianca's voice was filled with wonder. "Oh, Jason, you can't even begin to imagine how incredible it is. No sickness, no aging, nothing can hurt you. You'll be strong, and fast, and beautiful. You think you can swim now? Just think of how it will be when you've got the power and the speed of a vampire! You think your life is charmed here in DeVere Heights? It will be a hundred times better once you've transformed. You'll have wealth beyond your wildest dreams." Bianca's face had been changing as she spoke, and now it was glowing with an otherworldly beauty that astonished Jason. He'd never seen his aunt look so stunning.

That's her real face, he realized. *Her true vampire face.* Sienna had told him that the vampires toned down their natural beauty to fit in among humans. Clearly Aunt Bianca didn't think it mattered if Jason now saw her the way she really was.

She turned her luminous eyes on Sienna. "And once you've made the transformation, Jason, you and Sienna will be free to love each other," she said ecstatically.

"The transformation?" Jason said hesitantly. "What exactly—"

"No!" Sienna cut in. "You shouldn't even think about this, Jason." She turned to Bianca. "What if he doesn't *want* to transform? Anyway, the DeVere Heights Vampire Council would never allow it."

"The DeVere Heights Vampire Council answers to me," Bianca said dismissively. She narrowed her eyes at Sienna. "Why wouldn't Jason want to transform?" she asked, her voice suddenly as cold as the rain outside. "He'll have everything he's ever wanted."

"But he might—"

"That's enough!" Bianca snapped. Her blue eyes

had turned to stone. She turned and looked at Jason as if he were a bug under her shoe. "If you're not willing to transform, I'll simply tell Sienna's parents what I saw here today. They'll send her to France within twenty-four hours," she said flatly.

Jason's mouth dropped open in shock. What had happened to his aunt? One second she was alive with joy, gushing about the joys of being a vampire. The next she was threatening him.

"How can you say that?" he gasped. "Aunt Bianca—"

"It's time for Sienna to leave," she said.

Jason felt a stab of anger. Did she really think she could throw the girl he loved out of his own house? But Sienna's cheeks were pale. *She's scared,* Jason thought. *We were trying to keep the DeVere Heights Vampire Council from finding out about us, and now one of the* High *Council knows everything!*

Sienna let go of his hand. "I'll see you in school," she said quietly.

"Yeah," he replied. He smiled reassuringly, trying to cut through the worry that he saw in her eyes. But Sienna didn't smile back. She just shot a nervous glance at Bianca, turned, and hurried out into the rain.

"I don't like being threatened," Jason told his aunt, trying to control his anger.

Aunt Bianca laughed. "Don't be angry with me,

honey," she said, walking over to him. "I only want what's best for you." When she put her arm around him, Jason's shoulders tensed in spite of himself. She was still his aunt, but the way her personality seemed to flip from sweet to sour was starting to freak him out.

"There's simply no reason to even think twice about undergoing the transformation," Bianca went on conversationally. "I'm talking about money, power, prestige ... everything that I have. You know I have no children. You and Danielle are my closest family. You're my heirs."

Jason wasn't sure what to say. He'd never thought about this sort of thing before.

"But only a vampire can inherit my estate," Bianca continued. "You understand, don't you? Most of what I have belonged to my husband. He left me his position in the community. All his influence, his wealth—it was his legacy to me. And it will be my legacy to you—but it's a vampire's estate, and that's how it must remain."

"You're not sick or anything, are you?" Jason asked uncertainly. Why was she talking about inheritances?

"No." Bianca waved her hand dismissively. "I'm fine. I'm simply thinking about the future. At some point, you and Danielle will need to undergo the transformation. So why not now? If you became a vampire now, the Devereuxs will have no reason to object to your relationship with Sienna. It seems like perfect timing."

"I guess it does . . . ," Jason murmured, still trying to get his head around the idea.

But Aunt Bianca lit up as if he'd given his whole-hearted agreement. "You can't imagine how happy it will make me to see you join me as a vampire!" she cried, her eyes shining once again with that eerie light.

Jason ran his hand through his hair. "I can't believe you know," he murmured. "All this time, I thought you had no idea that I—"

"That you were aware of the vampires?" Aunt Bianca finished for him. "Well, I didn't know for a while. But once Sienna's parents told me about your heroics with Tamburo, I figured it out pretty quickly. How did you discover us?"

"When we first moved to Malibu, there was a vampire with the bloodlust," Jason said. "I fought with him. That's when I found out about the vampires."

"Hmm. I hadn't heard about that part," Bianca said with a little chuckle. "I knew about Luke Archer, of course, I just didn't know you were involved. But when Tyler stole the Lafrenières' chalice, you knew I was one of the vampires then, didn't you? You knew I was on the High Council."

Jason didn't answer. Just hearing her say Tyler's

name sent chills up his spine. The last time she'd spoken about Tyler, she'd been planning to kill him.

"You tricked me in order to save your friend," Bianca said lightly, reading his face, even though he hadn't said a word. Thankfully, she didn't seem angry.

"Yes." Jason took a deep breath. He was a little afraid to ask his next question, but he had to know. "Is Tyler safe now?"

Aunt Bianca rolled her eyes. "He's fine," she snapped, sounding irritated now. "As long as he minds his own business, he's inconsequential."

Jason frowned. One second Bianca seemed so warm, so much like her usual Aunt Bianca self. The next there was that *edge* again. He'd never seen his aunt so changeable before.

"Tyler never knew that the chalice belonged to vampires," Jason told her. "He had no idea—"

"Yeah, yeah, I heard the whole story." Bianca shook her head. "The stupid kid shouldn't have taken the chalice regardless."

"He was desperate," Jason argued. How dare she call Tyler stupid? "And besides, I got the chalice back."

"Right. Using money from your college fund. As if your parents weren't going to figure that out!" Bianca said harshly. "Luckily I found out in time to put the money back before they noticed."

"You did that?" Jason blurted.

"Who else?" Bianca asked. "I'm your aunt. I'll always be looking out for you."

That was kind of . . . creepy. The idea that Bianca kept such a close watch over him.

"Aren't you going to thank me?" Bianca asked, oozing sarcasm.

"Yes. Of course. Thanks," Jason said in a rush. Except it was hard to feel grateful for her help when she was being such a bitch.

"You're welcome. Now let's talk about something more interesting. Your future. As a vampire." She put her hand on his arm. "Think about it, Jason! You'll have long life, wealth, power. And you'll get to be with Sienna."

Her eyes were shining, and she wore a huge smile like a kid at Christmas. Jason just stared. She'd flipped back to Happy Bianca. This was more like the aunt he'd always known. More like the aunt he loved. Maybe it was just talking about Tyler that made her act strangely. Maybe she felt like she'd handled that situation badly.

Well, she did handle it badly, he thought. *And it makes me wonder how much I can trust her at all.* "I'm not sure," he said aloud. "I'll have to think about it. I mean, it's a pretty major decision."

"I guess it is." Bianca shrugged. "Okay, you take some time and mull it over. I have other things to attend to in the meantime." She grabbed her umbrella.

"Wait," Jason said. "What about Dani? Have you talked to her about this?" *Please say no,* he pleaded silently. Dani was so besotted with Ryan right now, and so in awe of Aunt Bianca all the time, that she'd probably jump at the chance to become a vampire without a second thought.

"Of course not," Bianca said, stepping out into the rain without opening her umbrella. "I think Danielle would find it a little odd, considering that she doesn't even know vampires exist!" She stood there talking to him, seemingly unaware of the rain soaking through her hair and clothes.

"Um, right," Jason answered. "Aunt Bianca, you're getting wet."

Bianca glanced up and seemed to notice the rain for the first time. "Oh, I'd better run inside, then. We'll talk about this again soon." She gave him a little wave and dashed for the main house.

Jason watched her go, frowning. He wasn't sure what to think. At least his aunt didn't know about Dani and Ryan yet, so he could weigh the pros and cons of becoming a vampire without having to worry about his sister.

Wait, Jason said to himself. *Am I actually considering this?* Was he really thinking about becoming a vampire? His heart beat faster at the very thought of it. To be like Sienna or Zach, to have that kind of power—it was an incredible idea.

So why did he have such an uneasy feeling about this? Why did he feel a strange reluctance to go through with it? Why did everything about Bianca and her suggestion make his brain scream, "Danger!"?

THIRTEEN

"Bee!" Jason heard his mother squeal half an hour later. "You didn't tell me you were coming!"

Jason got up and made his way into the house. He'd hung in the pool house until the rain stopped, but that hadn't been nearly enough time to come to any conclusions about Aunt Bianca's suggestion.

In the kitchen, Mrs. Freeman was hugging her sister.

"I only found out this morning that I have a meeting in L.A. this week," Bianca said. "My new assistant keeps messing up my calendar. I never know where I'm supposed to be."

Jason's dad frowned. "I didn't know you had a new assistant."

"What happened to Jacinda?" Mrs. Freeman asked.

Bianca shrugged. "I fired her."

"Why?"

"Because I wanted to," Bianca snapped. She turned toward Jason and smiled. "Here's our swimming sensation!"

"Um . . . hi, Aunt Bianca," he said. Was he supposed to pretend he hadn't seen her already today?

He could see why she'd want to keep their conversation in the pool house private.

"Where is my beautiful niece?" Bianca asked.

"She went out with some friends," Mrs. Freeman said. "Who was it again, Jason? Kristy and Billy?"

He wasn't sure what to say. Dani was with Ryan, but obviously his parents didn't know that. And he didn't want to mention Ryan's name in front of Bianca. She'd know Ryan was a vampire, and it wouldn't take her long to figure out that Dani knew it too. Still, he hated lying to his mom. "I'm not sure," he fudged. "I didn't see her leave."

Mr. Freeman took out his cell phone. "I'll give her a call," he said. "I'm sure she'll want to come right home when she finds out you're here, Bianca."

"It's true. She worships you," Jason's mom said. "Everything *you* do, *she* wants to do."

Bianca shot Jason a secret smile. He pretended not to see. That was exactly what he was afraid of: that Dani would turn herself into a vampire just to be like her aunt. And that was not a good enough reason to make such a drastic decision. *Do I have a good enough reason?* he wondered. He was in love with Sienna. But was that enough?

Dani arrived home about ten minutes later, just as Jason was sitting down to banana splits with his parents and Bianca.

"Aunt Bee?" Danielle called the second she stepped in the front door.

Bianca jumped up and held out her arms as Dani bounded into the dining room and flung herself into the hug. "What are you doing here?" Dani cried happily. "Where have you been lately? I've missed you so much!"

"That's true. You haven't told us why you've been out of touch," Mrs. Freeman put in. "I was starting to get worried, Bee."

"Look at your hair," Bianca gasped, grabbing a lock of Danielle's dark red hair. "You changed the color."

"Yeah, I went a little darker. Do you like it?" Dani asked. "It's almost as dark as yours, now that I look at it. Just with more red highlights."

"I told her I didn't want her coloring her hair," Mrs. Freeman said.

"Oh, Mom, everybody at school does it," Dani retorted. "You should see Kristy—hers is practically black now! This will wash out in a few weeks, though, don't worry."

"But your natural color is so pretty," Jason's mom said wistfully. "But let's get back to you, Bianca. Where have you been?"

"You know. Here and there." Bianca waved her hand dismissively. "Nowhere interesting. I'd much rather hear your gossip. Any new boyfriends, Danielle?"

Jason nearly choked on a piece of banana. "Aunt

Bianca, you're not allowed to ask that!" he said quickly. He didn't want her getting into Ryan territory.

Thankfully, Dani backed him up. "Yeah. Love life gossip is off-limits." She laughed.

"At least while we're around, right?" Mr. Freeman joked.

"And I want to hear about you, Bee," Mrs. Freeman insisted. "I called your apartment in New York a dozen times. And I kept leaving messages with Jacinda."

"I told you Jacinda was hopeless. That's why I fired her," Bianca said breezily. "I'll have to check that the answering machine is working at home, I guess."

"Do you have any new celebrity sightings to tell me about?" Dani asked.

"Tons," Bianca replied. "I've been casting a remake of *Saturday Night Fever*, so I have lots of gorgeous guys coming in to audition."

"They're remaking *Saturday Night Fever*?" Jason asked. "That's a terrible idea!"

Aunt Bianca shrugged. "I don't come up with these ideas, I only cast them. And you wouldn't believe how much bad dancing I've had to sit through."

"That's my cue to leave," Jason said. "Hearing about actors is bad enough. I don't want to know about them trying to dance." He stood up. "I'm going to get some work done on my Faulkner paper."

As he climbed up the stairs, he heard Bianca

continuing her casting story. *Looks like she finally found a way to make Mom stop asking where she's been,* he thought. He couldn't help but wonder why his aunt was so reluctant to talk about herself on this visit. Usually she was more than happy to tell them all about what she'd been up to.

Jason shook his head. Would he ever be able to stop thinking this way: as if everything Aunt Bianca did was suspicious somehow? He doubted it. She'd been willing to kill Tyler—a kid she'd known since he was little.

I'll try to forget about it, Jason promised himself. *I'll try to focus on the future, like Bianca said. She is my aunt, after all, and I know she loves us.* But then he remembered the look in her eyes when he had argued with her about Tyler. *At least, I think she does. . . .*

When Jason arrived at the breakfast table the next morning, his mother was already grilling Bianca.

". . . but I don't understand. You have your cell phone with you all the time. Why haven't you been answering?" Mrs. Freeman asked quietly.

"I'm very busy, Tania." Bianca replied, sounding annoyed. Last night, she'd avoided his mother's questions, but she couldn't keep doing that forever. Jason hovered in the doorway, wondering if he should go back upstairs. He didn't want to interrupt.

"Too busy for your family? Too busy to just let me know you're okay?" Mrs. Freeman pressed.

"Yes!" Bianca snapped, standing up abruptly and going to refill her coffee cup.

"Well, that's not acceptable, Bee," Mrs. Freeman said, sounding annoyed herself. "What could possibly be keeping you so busy that you'd act so inconsiderately?"

Jason turned to go, but the movement caught Bianca's eye. "Jason!" she cried in a relieved voice. "Good morning! Want some coffee? I can make more."

With a grimace, Jason spun back around. "I'm sorry. I didn't mean to barge in on you guys," he said.

"Nonsense. We're not talking about anything important," Aunt Bianca said. But Jason saw his mother's eyes flash, and knew she wasn't thrilled that he'd shown up when he did.

"Okay. Well, I'm just going to grab a granola bar and head back upstairs," Jason said. That way, he could get in and out of the kitchen quickly and leave his mother and Aunt Bianca to talk.

"Absolutely not. That isn't a good breakfast. And besides, I'm not here very often," Bianca said. "I want to see as much as I can of you and Danielle."

"Who's talking about me?" Dani called from the stairs. "You better be saying nice things!"

So much for letting Mom have a private talk with Bianca, Jason thought. He headed for the fridge to see if there was any steak left over from yesterday's lunch. Why have a granola bar if he didn't have to?

"Morning," Dani said, padding into the kitchen in jeans and a T-shirt, with bunny slippers on her feet.

"Hi, sweetie," Aunt Bianca practically sang. "Sleep well?"

"I guess . . ." Dani went straight for the coffee pot. She wasn't a morning person.

"You were telling me what you've been busy doing, Bianca," Mrs. Freeman reminded her. Jason shot his mother a surprised look. Obviously she wasn't going to drop the subject just because Aunt Bianca preferred to talk with him and Dani.

Bianca sighed. "I'm working, all right? Why do you care so much?"

"Because I'm your sister," Mrs. Freeman said. "And I'm worried about you. First you drop out of sight and don't return calls. Then you show up looking tense and exhausted. And, strangest of all, when I spoke to Jacinda before you let her go, she told me you'd been insisting that everyone talk only in French! What is going on, Bee?"

"Nothing. I'm fine. Everything's fine," Bianca said shortly.

"But—"

"Come on, Dani," Bianca suddenly cried, jumping up from the table. "Let's hit Melrose."

Dani's eyes went wide and she put her mug down. "Seriously?" She glanced at her mother to see if it was okay, since they were obviously mid-argument here. Mrs. Freeman sighed loudly and nodded at Dani.

"Yup, let's go," Bianca said. "We'll be there when the stores open and we'll stay all day. There's a new restaurant at the corner of Melrose and La Brea that I want to try, so we can do lunch there. And one of the vintage shops is holding a dress for me."

She was already heading for the door.

"Let me throw on some shoes," Dani said, racing for the stairs.

"Hurry," Bianca said impatiently. She stopped at the table in the foyer and glanced into the mirror on the wall.

"Bianca." Jason thought his mother sounded annoyed, but she forced a smile. "How long are you staying in California this time?"

"I'm not sure yet," Bianca said, running her fingers through her hair. She frowned at her reflection, and ran her fingers through again. Then again. Jason wasn't sure why; her hair looked fine.

"Ready!" Dani clomped down the stairs in a pair of wedge-heeled shoes.

Bianca was still trying to fix her hair. "Do you have a brush, Danielle?"

"Sure." Dani pulled a hairbrush out of her bag and handed it over. "But your hair looks perfect."

Aunt Bianca didn't answer. She took the brush, flipped her head upside down, and brushed out her long dark hair. Then she stood upright, checked the mirror again, and nodded with satisfaction. "Okay, I'm ready. See you later, everyone." She grabbed her keys and headed out the door, Dani on her heels.

Jason looked at his mother. She was staring after her sister with a concerned expression on her face. "Mom?" he said. "You okay?"

"I'm fine," she replied. "But I don't think Bianca is."

"She just has a lot on her mind," Jason assured her. "I'm sure she's okay."

"I hope you're right," Mrs. Freeman said, starting to clear away the breakfast dishes. Jason sat down and finished eating in silence, deep in thought. He knew what Aunt Bianca had on her mind: his transformation. It was preying on his mind too.

All night long he'd had dreams about Sienna. Sometimes they were bad—he and she were being torn apart from each other—sometimes they were good, and, once, he'd been drinking blood. That was the dream that had woken him. He had to admit that it had made him feel kind of nauseated. The thought of drinking blood was sickening. But it was also the only bad thing he could think of about being a vampire.

Otherwise it sounded like a pretty good deal. The vampires in DeVere Heights were rich, powerful, and stronger than any human. Besides which they could heal with incredible speed, change their appearance, and live for hundreds of years. All in all, it was good to be a vampire.

And it's not as if they just sit around thinking about how cool they are, Jason thought. *The vampire families do all kinds of charity work.* It was likely that Jason would be able to do more good in his life if he were a vampire than if he remained an ordinary human.

Aunt Bianca thinks it's the right thing to do, Jason reminded himself. Yeah, his aunt had been acting kind of bitchy lately. But she was the one who had put the money back in Jason's account. That proved that she was looking out for him. And didn't he owe her something for that?

Most important of all was Sienna. If he were a vampire, he could be with Sienna. There would be no more obstacles between them.

"Honey, I'm going to check on your father," Mrs. Freeman said, interrupting Jason's thoughts. "He's been working all morning and he hasn't had his coffee." She carelessly tousled his hair as she walked by, heading upstairs with a steaming coffee mug.

As his mother disappeared up the steps, Jason sighed. He'd just realized the biggest downside to becoming a vampire. It wasn't drinking blood—he could probably get used to that, given enough time. It was his parents. His mom and dad weren't about to turn vampire. He probably wouldn't even be allowed to tell them what he'd become. How could he do something that would set him apart from his own parents in such a drastic way?

It's not as if I've decided yet, he reminded himself. *I have to talk it through with Sienna first anyway.* She hadn't seemed that thrilled with the idea when Bianca had mentioned it yesterday. Was that all about her parents' opposition? Or was there another reason she didn't want him to become like her? Did she just not want him to make such a big change *only* to be with her? And if he decided to do it, would it be mostly for her? Even Jason wasn't sure about that.

The phone rang, making him jump. Jason tipped his chair back on two legs so he could reach the cordless on the counter. "Hello?"

"Bonjour. C'est Adam," said Adam. "Am I interrupting anything?"

"Yes, and thank you," Jason replied. "I was making myself insane."

"Insane about what?"

"Oh . . ." Jason hesitated. "My aunt, who's willing to kill people, wants me to become a vampire like her" wasn't the kind of thing you just blurted out over the phone. "I'll tell you about it later," he said finally.

"Cool. So listen, it's time for more French practice,"

Adam declared. He lowered his voice and added quietly, "If you know what I mean."

"Well, what I think you mean is that it's time for more French practice," Jason replied.

"That's right, my crafty friend," Adam whispered. "Frrrrench practice."

Adam was being unusually cryptic—even by Adam's standards. "What's up?" Jason asked, intrigued.

"Nothing," Adam said in his normal voice. "So meet me at the Getty Center."

"The Getty Center?"

"Yup. At noon," Adam said. "In front of the doors."

"Why are we going to the Getty Center for French tutoring?" Jason asked.

"Because you suck at French," Adam replied. "Duh. See you there." He hung up.

Jason stared at the phone for a few seconds, then hit the off button. Adam was being bizarre. But Adam was always kind of bizarre, and Jason needed a break from his vampire thoughts. It would be good to get out of the house for a while, and he'd never been to the Getty Center.

An hour later, Jason was riding the monorail up the steep hill to the museum. He'd had to leave the Bug down below in the parking garage, and now it felt as if he were riding a futuristic train to some sci-fi city. Everything was made of some kind of beige stone, and the whole place looked as if it had simply grown out of the mountain. When he got off the monorail, he just stood still for a moment, looking around. The Getty Center was a little above him, up a series of wide, shallow steps. Beige steps. He could already see Adam at the top, moonwalking back and forth for Jason's amusement.

Jason shook his head and jogged up the steps. "This place is outrageous," he said.

"Say that in French," Adam replied.

"I don't know how."

"Neither do I," Adam admitted. "But, yeah, it's pretty cool. I always think this is what everything will look like once we colonize the moon. It's very *2001: A Space Odyssey*."

"If you say so," Jason replied. "So is there French art here or something?"

Adam gazed at him blankly.

"Art?" Jason repeated. "Inside the museum? And French, for the French practice?"

"No, are you crazy?" Adam said. "Let's go out to the gardens. The museum is lame. This place is all about two things and two things only: the architecture and the views." He led Jason through a couple of sets of glass doors and out through the other side of the stone building. A green lawn and a huge garden lay spread out before them. There were more stone buildings surrounding it—classrooms or something, Jason assumed. They were beige too.

A quick movement near one of the buildings caught Jason's eye. He squinted into the sun. A door was just closing, but he could swear he'd seen somebody there just a second before. Watching him.

"See? Ocean," Adam said, pointing to the right. "And that way, city." He pointed to the left.

Jason peered at the blue horizon, then at the smoggy gray buildings of Los Angeles. "Wow," he said. "You can see pretty much everything from up here."

"Now you understand, young apprentice," Adam said. "It's a rockin' place, and the café makes a mean mozzarella and tomato sandwich."

"And we're here . . . why?" Jason asked.

"Because it's far from the listening ears of Malibu," Adam informed him. "The listening vampiric, *parental* ears of Malibu."

"Oh," Jason said. *"Oh!"* Now he got it. They weren't here for French lessons—they were here because Adam had a message for him. From Sienna.

"Slow on the uptake, aren't you?" Adam teased. "Here I am being all cryptic and you don't even notice."

"Sorry. I thought you were just being you. I usually only understand about a third of what you say on a good day," Jason said. "So what's up?"

"I got a phone call from the lovely Sienna this

morning," Adam said. "She wants to see you. Tonight. She's seriously nervous about her parents, isn't she?"

"Yeah. Why?"

"She kept going on and on about how I couldn't put anything in writing. No sending you e-mails or text messages or even good old-fashioned notes. She even made me promise not to talk about it on the phone with you."

"So that's why we had to meet somewhere?" Jason guessed.

"Yeah." Adam's hazel eyes were serious. "She doesn't really think her parents have your phone bugged, does she?"

"I don't know," Jason said. "That seems crazy. But . . ."

"But the fact that the toothy ones exist at all is crazy," Adam finished for him. "Right. Better not to take chances."

Jason glanced back over at the door to the class-room building. "Yeah. Listen, did Sienna say what she wants?" Jason asked.

"I kind of assumed you'd know that," Adam said, wiggling his eyebrows suggestively.

Jason ignored that. "Where am I supposed to meet her?"

"At the observatory in Griffith Park," Adam said. "It's far from home and it's in the middle of nowhere. Too bad it's not still closed for renovations—that would have made it an extra good rendezvous point, although the new Leonard Nimoy Event Horizon is awesome. Anyway, you guys should be safe from Sienna's parents there. Plus, it's an excellent make-out spot. Or so I've heard. It's in lots of movies."

"What time?"

"Nine o'clock." Adam's face broke into a grin. "This is so cloak-and-dagger! I should do a movie about it— part thriller, part romance. All good."

The door of the classroom building inched open again, and a guy slid out, his eyes on Jason. But this time, Jason's eyes were on him, too—and Jason recognized him: It was the goateed guy from the speedboat, and the pier.

Jason's blood seemed to freeze in his veins. They stared at each other for a moment, then Goatee slipped quickly back inside the building.

"Time to go," Jason said grimly.

"What? Why?" Adam trailed after him as Jason rushed back through the museum toward the main entrance. "I was only kidding about the movie—"

"We're being hunted," Jason told him quickly. "Remember our friend with the stupid goatee?"

"Who could forget?" Adam replied.

"He's here."

Adam stopped in his tracks. "But there are no toothies here," he said. "There's just you and me. You don't think he could've assumed that we're V, do you?" He sounded frightened. After all, Jason had nearly been killed by the last hunter who'd thought he was a vampire.

"Keep moving. We need to get back down to the parking garage," Jason said. "I'll recognize his car. Maybe we can follow him."

Adam pointed to the monorail stop. "There's a train about to leave. Let's go." They ran for the monorail, squeezing through the doors just as they were closing.

Jason did a quick scan of the car. No Goatee. "I'm confused," he said. "This is twice I've seen the dude when I wasn't with Sienna. Is he looking for her, or looking for me?"

"And if he's found you, why hasn't he taken a shot?" Adam murmured.

Jason didn't know the answer. They rode in silence the rest of the way. The monorail doors slid open in the parking garage, and they hurried out. The museum wasn't too crowded today, and the parking attendants had directed all traffic to park on the same level. Adam kept watch for Goatee while Jason jogged up and down the line of cars, looking for the black Mercedes.

"There!" he said, spotting it behind an enormous Escalade.

Adam ran over and studied the Mercedes. "Are you sure it's this one?" he asked.

"I got a pretty good look at it from the fishing pier," Jason said. "Okay, let's get the Bug. When he comes down to the car, we'll be ready to follow."

But Adam was shaking his head. "Sometimes, my friend, I think I've been gifted with all this brilliance just so I can help you in your quest for . . . What *are* you questing for, anyway?"

Jason just stared at him.

"Right. Sorry. What I mean is, we don't have to follow him. As if he wouldn't notice your silly VW in his rearview anyway!" Adam said.

"What do you mean?" Jason asked.

"If you look closely at the bumper of this car, you'll see a sticker with a D and a circle and a little triangle-type thing," Adam pointed out.

"So?"

"So that is a parking permit for the DeVere Center," Adam said. "Only employees are allowed to park in that lot."

Jason's eyes widened. "Are you telling me that this guy works at the blood research center?"

"I'm telling you he works for Sienna's father— who runs the blood research center," Adam said. "Although I'm guessing that the only research our goateed friend does is research into Sienna's boyfriend and his activities!"

"I can't believe it," Jason said. "They actually have

somebody following me just to make sure I stay away from her! That's insane."

"On the up side, at least now we can keep your meeting with Sienna tonight a secret," Adam said, then raised his eyebrows. "Go ahead, ask me how."

"How?"

"Well, if you'll look back at this lovely Devereux-mobile, you'll note that the license plate has a registration sticker on it."

Jason glanced at the plate. "So what?"

"It's expired," Adam grinned. "See what you learn to look for when your father's a cop? I'll call in the expired registration just as you leave tonight. The police will pull him over to give him a ticket, and you'll have the time you need to lose him."

"Wow!" Jason said. "Maybe you could have a career in espionage movies. Thanks, man."

"Your eternal worship is the only thanks I need," Adam told him, leading the way back to the Bug.

Jason slid behind the wheel, feeling hopeful for the first time in days. Tonight he'd see Sienna.

And nobody would catch them.

FOURTEEN

The parking lot of the observatory was dark when Jason pulled in. He cut the engine and turned off his headlights, but left the roof of the Bug up. Even though Adam was taking care of Goatee, it didn't hurt to be careful. He didn't want to risk being seen with Sienna, and sitting in a convertible with the top down was a good way to be seen.

There were a few cars scattered around the parking lot. Maybe the other people were here to see the view, which was definitely something to see. The observatory was set up high in the hills near the Hollywood sign, and the city lay spread out beneath it. The lights of the L.A. streets stretched out in front of him like the neon spokes of a giant Ferris wheel. Still, Jason guessed that the people in the other cars were probably too busy making out to look at the view.

By the time he heard the car door open, Sienna was already sitting next to him. He smiled. She could move fast when she wanted to. If he were to become a vampire, he'd be able to do that, too.

"One of your father's security guys followed me,"

he told her. "It was the goateed guy from the speed-boat, remember him?"

Sienna nodded. "So those guys were spies for my dad!" she fumed.

"Don't sweat it. Adam helped me lose him," Jason told her. He grinned. "And probably got him a traffic ticket in the process."

"Good," Sienna laughed. Then she sighed. "We can't get caught, Jason. If I have to go to France, we'll *never* get to see each other."

He took her hand, twining his fingers through hers. "I won't let that happen. Maybe I should just do what my aunt Bianca says. I think she really does want what's best for me. I found out she was the one who put the money back in my college account. She—"

"No, you can't do it!" Sienna cut him off. "That's why I had to see you tonight, to tell you I don't want you to try and become a vampire."

"But if I did, we could be together," he began.

"You don't know what a huge risk it is," Sienna cut in. "Did your aunt tell you what could happen?"

"No. What do you mean?"

"Jason. It's not a simple little thing, for a human to turn into a vampire," Sienna said, her tone serious. "There's a reason the High Council forbids it. And not just because it brings the vampire and human worlds too close together." She drew a deep breath.

"One of the reasons we don't like humans to turn is that they could die."

Her words hit Jason like a splash of ice water. "Die?"

"Yes. The transformation is very difficult. Sometimes humans just can't handle it. Their . . . your genetic structure is different from ours. For some humans, it's fine and they become vampires with no trouble. They have our powers, our long life, everything we have. They become just like us."

"Right," Jason said. "That's what I could be."

"Yes, but not necessarily," Sienna corrected him. "Some humans become . . . well, they become . . . unstable. Physically. Their bodies break down. They die."

Jason took a deep breath. "That doesn't sound good."

"That's not the worst thing," Sienna said. "Believe me, the incompatible ones who die are lucky compared to the ones who live. When a human is unable to handle the transformation, we don't always know right away."

"But you said—"

"I said sometimes they die. But sometimes they go mad."

Jason frowned. "Go mad how?"

"A long, slow descent into insanity," Sienna explained, her voice trembling as she spoke. "It doesn't show for a long time, years even. Everything seems fine. The turned vampire has powers and long life and the whole deal. But then something happens. They start hallucinating sometimes. Or they become violent. Sometimes they even succumb to the bloodlust—and you know what that's like."

Jason nodded, remembering the glowing green eyes of Luke Archer, the bloodlusting vampire he'd fought back when he'd first moved to Malibu. There had been nothing human about Luke. Nothing sane. He'd been a monster.

"It's not just bloodlust," Sienna went on. "Sometimes there's extreme dementia. One turned vampire in France went so crazy that she began feeding off herself. She thought she was drinking the blood of a human, but she was really drinking her own blood. They found her dead of starvation."

Jason swallowed hard. The image was disturbing.

"And there was a vampire in New York with the transformation sickness who had such extreme delusions that they had to put him in a mental institution. Think about that. We live for centuries, Jason, so the High Council had to find a way to kill him, otherwise the doctors would have noticed that he wasn't getting old like he was supposed to."

"So he was murdered?"

"Yes. To protect the other vampires."

"It might have been better that way," Jason said. "He was insane. And he would have had to live that way for *hundreds* of years!"

"Exactly." Sienna clung to his hand. "It's a horrible fate. Not only to go mad, but to descend deeper and deeper into insanity over such a long period. Jason, do you see why I can't let you take that risk?"

He nodded slowly. Dying or going mad. Those were pretty bad side effects. Why hadn't Aunt Bianca mentioned them?

"Anyway, transforming is not something you even have to consider right now," Sienna went on. "I mean, we're young. There's no rush. We have plenty of time to make life choices like that. If we're still together in ten years, you can decide then."

He pulled her closer and kissed her, letting his lips linger on hers. "We'll still be together," he murmured.

Sienna pulled back. "But what are we going to do about Bianca? If you tell her you're not going to undergo the transformation right now, won't she tell my parents about us? She seemed so insistent that it's something you have to do right away. I don't get that."

"She wants Dani to transform right now too," Jason told her. "She was talking about her legacy and how we'd have to be vampires to inherit from her. I guess she just wants it done—so she can be sure that we're her vampire heirs, or something. I mean, once

Dani and I transform, there's no going back, is there?"

"No, that's true," Sienna said thoughtfully. "But what are we going to do? How long do you think she'll give us before she goes to my parents?"

"She's my aunt. She loves me. I'll just tell her I'm considering transforming into a vampire. I think she'll be satisfied with that for a while," Jason answered, hoping it was true.

"Right." Sienna relaxed. "Good. Then it's settled." She pulled her bag onto her lap and dug around inside. "I brought you a treat."

"Just being with you is a treat," Jason said.

She laughed. "Aren't you a smoothie?" she teased. "Look!" She took a Tootsie Pop from her bag and handed it to him, then pulled out another one for herself.

"Candy on a stick," Jason said, chuckling.

"We have a long tradition of foods on sticks," Sienna said, unwrapping her lollipop.

Jason opened his, too, remembering the afternoon they'd spent at the mall. They were Christmas shopping, and he'd introduced Sienna to the concept of the corn dog at the food court. They'd been officially just friends then, and it was one of the best times they'd ever had together. He held up his Tootsie Pop in a toast. "Here's to you and me," he said. "And our friendship."

Sienna ceremoniously tapped her Tootsie Pop against his, then stuck it in her mouth. Jason did the same, and for a moment they just sat silently, looking at the view. "We've been through a lot together," Sienna murmured finally.

He nodded. "And we'll get through this as well. Somehow. Your parents can't keep us apart forever."

"We have to be careful," Sienna said. "I'll stay in touch with you through Adam. But I'd better get going now." She glanced out the car window, her brow furrowed. "I know you weren't followed, but I still can't shake the feeling that they'll find us somehow."

"What did you tell your dad?"

"I said I was going to a club in Hollywood, so I have to put in an appearance there."

Jason nodded thoughtfully. "Hmm, that means that Goatee will probably have gone there when the cops finished ticketing him. He'll be looking for me, but he'll only see you. It's perfect!"

Sienna grinned, reached over, and kissed him lightly on the forehead. "I'll see you in school." Then she was gone, and Jason was alone with the view.

He pulled out his cell and started to dial Adam's number, then stopped. He wanted to get his friend's take on the whole vampire transformation thing. Adam was good at making decisions. He always had lists of pros and cons, and he managed to think of things in a slightly skewed way that helped to give Jason a new perspective. But how could Adam help him here, really? Jason knew there was no real decision to make. Sienna was right: It was too big a risk to take right now. It was too big a decision to rush. There was no harm in waiting.

Except for the part where he couldn't be with Sienna while he was a human. Which made him consider the risks all over again. . . .

FIFTEEN

When the alarm clock went off on Monday morning, Jason was already awake. He'd been tossing and turning all night, thinking about the vampire transformation. It sounded like pretty scary stuff. But how often did the transformation go wrong? What percentage of the time did it work perfectly? He should have asked Sienna those questions.

Jason dragged himself out of bed, exhausted. He figured a nice cold shower would wake him right up, so he padded down the hallway to the bathroom and pushed open the door.

Bianca stood inside, her face about an inch from the mirror. She was concentrating so hard that she didn't notice him behind her. Jason started to leave, but not before he saw what she was doing: plucking her eyebrows. To be more exact, plucking *every single hair* from her eyebrows. One after the other. Already one of her eyebrows was entirely gone.

That was not normal.

Jason slowly backed out of the bathroom. *Whoa,* he thought. *Mom's right after all. Something freaky is going on with Aunt Bianca.*

All through breakfast Jason kept an eye on his aunt. She'd drawn her eyebrows in with some kind of makeup and she was acting normal, just eating and reading the paper. On the drive to school, he glanced over at Dani, who was frantically trying to finish her reading for English.

"Is there some new fad where you pluck out your whole eyebrow?" he asked.

Dani didn't glance up from her book. "Why? You planning to try out a new look?"

"Aunt Bianca was doing it this morning."

That got her attention. "Aunt Bee? Really? Maybe it is a new fad." She thought for a moment. "There were some old-time movie stars who did that. Shaved off their eyebrows and drew in new ones with eyebrow pencil. They got the perfect shape they wanted that way."

She kept reading. But Jason was still worried.

"How was shopping yesterday?" he asked.

Dani dropped her book into her lap. "Well, I got this great new pair of jeans. They're distressed, but not *too* distressed, you know?"

"I *meant*, how was Aunt Bianca?"

"She was fine, Jason. What's this all about?"

"She's just being a little weird, I think," he said. "She's so moody and she doesn't want to tell Mom why."

"Yeah, she was kinda moody yesterday," Danielle said thoughtfully. "At one store, she actually made the salesgirl cry."

"How?"

"Oh, Aunt Bianca wanted these shoes and the only ones they had in her size were scuffed. So she had a little tantrum and she called the girl a wannabe. I felt bad for the girl."

"That really doesn't sound like Aunt Bianca," Jason pointed out.

"I guess not." Dani frowned. "It's pretty typical Hollywood behavior, though. And Aunt Bianca has been working in Hollywood for a while. Maybe it's rubbing off. She does seem very stressed about work."

"That's true," Jason said. "And she's not dating or anything. Between losing Stefan and having this high-pressure career, she's probably at the end of her rope. She needs a vacation."

"I know! I'll tell Mom to invite Bianca to a spa week. That's totally relaxing. They could just drive out to Palm Springs or something. It's perfect!" Dani picked up her book, a big grin on her face. "I'm such a genius."

Jason let her read for the rest of the drive. His mind went back to the question of becoming a vampire or not. He couldn't really think about anything else. What would it be like, to know you were going to live for a couple of hundred years? To not worry about sickness or injury?

He turned the VW into the parking lot at DeVere High and found a spot next to Brad's Jeep.

"There's Belle," Dani said, peering at the vintage Beemer two spaces away. She slammed her book shut, stuffed it in her bag, and jumped out of the car without a glance at Jason. "Belle!" she yelled. "What up, homegirl?"

Belle laughed. "Come here. I found the ideal shade of brown lipstick for you yesterday. As soon as I saw it, I thought of you. . . ."

Jason climbed out of the car as Dani and Belle walked off toward the school.

"When did they become such good friends?" Adam asked, coming up behind him.

"Since Ryan Patrick," Jason replied. "And palling around with Dani helps take Belle's mind off of Dom."

Adam nodded. "So, what are you up to tonight?"

"Why?"

"Because, *mon ami*, I have something to show you. Something you really want to see."

"ParanormalPI.com?" Jason asked later that evening.

"That's what I said," Adam replied, tossing Jason's Nerf basketball at the hoop attached to the bedroom door.

Jason typed the web address into his computer and watched as a serious-looking site appeared. "It looks like a college information page or something."

"Well, yeah, it *looks* all scholarly. And it is compared to most of the vampire websites. But there's still a lot of trash. Check out the titles of the articles in the archive," Adam told him.

Jason took a closer look. "'Ghost gives accurate information on Mississippi shootings'."

"Oh, that one was cool," Adam said, tossing the ball again. "This ghost communicated with the homicide detective through his iPod."

"'Woman gives birth to flying fish'," Jason read dubiously.

"Like I said—a lot of trash." Adam threw himself down on Jason's bed. "But it's a pretty good site even so. They investigate every paranormal story they find in the tabloids, and a lot of them are really hilarious. One or two even turn out to be true—in one way or another."

"Okay. So why am I interested in this?"

"Um . . . because you're dating a vampire?" Adam said.

"We're just friends," Jason corrected him.

"Yes. And I'm a world-champion bodybuilder," Adam replied, deadpan. "So do you want to see the vampire-interest story or not?"

"I guess so."

"Search for 'vampire' in the database."

Jason typed in "vampire" and hit enter. The first link that popped up was entitled "Priceless Vampire Artifact for Sale." He clicked on it.

"'A Malibu, California pawnshop is offering an antique chalice for sale to the highest bidder,'" he read aloud. "'This is no worthless trophy cup. This is a valuable piece of art that is linked with several legendary vampire rituals. Blood sacrifices, undead wedding ceremonies, and vampire initiation are only a few of the sacraments rumored to have been performed with this beautiful chalice.'"

Jason stopped reading. "Well, they got *one* of the rituals right." The chalice had definitely been used to initiate Zach Lafrenière into the DeVere Heights Vampire Council.

"I'm thinking this is where our not-so-friendly neighborhood vampire-hunter got his lead on the DeVere Heights toothies," Adam said. "Tamburo probably lurked on sites like this all the time. He saw the notice about the chalice, he came straight to Malibu to find out whether it was a real vampire artifact or not. Because where there's an ancient vampire chalice, there are likely to be vampires to kill."

Jason nodded, his face grim. "I wonder how many other vampire hunters do the same thing."

"And I wonder how the website even heard about the chalice," Adam replied.

"That pawnbroker probably put it on this site to advertise it," Jason said. "It's a site for supernatural enthusiasts, after all." He closed the page, and the "vampire" search results filled the screen again.

"Yeah, I guess saying that it was mysterious and all that would get some publicity and drive the price higher," Adam agreed.

But Jason barely heard him. His attention was on another link down toward the bottom of the search page: "Blood Research Center Creates Top Secret Vampire Test." Jason clicked on it.

He'd only read about three sentences before he knew he had to call Sienna. Immediately. He reached for the phone, then stopped. Sienna had been worried about his calls being monitored. "Can I borrow your cell?" he asked Adam.

Adam handed it to him, then came to read the web page over Jason's shoulder. Jason dialed Sienna's number.

"Hello?" she answered. "Adam?"

"No, it's me," Jason said. "Can you talk? It's important."

"Yes. My parents are out at a meeting. Are you okay?"

"I'm reading an article online. It mentions the DeVere Center for Advanced Genetics and Blood

Research. Your father is on the board of that place, right?"

"Right," Sienna said. "Why?"

"This article says that research scientists there have devised a DNA test to determine whether a human could secretly be a vampire without knowing it," Jason told her.

"That's ridiculous," Adam said.

"That *is* ridiculous," Sienna put in.

"Well, yeah, obviously it's been exaggerated," Jason agreed. "I think it would be pretty hard not to notice yourself drinking blood. But a few of the other articles on this site have a grain of truth to them. It's possible that this one does too."

"Okay . . . ," Sienna said slowly.

"We were talking about genetics yesterday," Jason reminded her. "If the DeVere Center is doing any research on vampire genetics, it might be useful to us."

"The center e-mails my father every week with progress reports," Sienna said. "Just to keep him up to date on their latest research."

"Can you find those e-mails?"

"I'll try. But it has to be fast. My parents will be home any minute." Jason heard Sienna moving around as she spoke. "Dad's computer is downstairs, in his study."

"Put it on speaker. I can't tell what's happening," Adam complained.

Jason set the cell phone on his desk and hit the speaker button.

"Okay, I'm at the computer," Sienna's voice came through the tiny speaker. "I just have to log on as my dad."

"Do you know his password?" Adam asked.

"Yup. It's my middle name," Sienna replied. "Genevieve." Jason heard the keys tapping as she typed. A little bell sound announced that she was logged in. "I'm going to his e-mail," she narrated. Then she groaned.

"What?" Jason and Adam asked together.

"There are hundreds of them," Sienna explained.

"How many from the DeVere Center?" Adam said.

Jason quickly scanned his computer screen for the date of the article on ParanormalPI.com. "This piece is from last week, so check the last couple of months."

"This is weird. I don't see any e-mail from the DeVere Center, but there should be a bunch," Sienna told him.

"Go Dumpster diving," Adam suggested.

"What?" Sienna asked.

"I think I can translate," Jason offered. "Check the recycle bin for deleted messages."

Sienna was silent for a moment, then Jason heard her gasp.

"What?" he asked.

"Yeah, the suspense is killing me," Adam agreed. "Especially since I don't know what we're talking about."

"Okay, this is an e-mail from a couple of weeks ago," Sienna said. "Apparently there was an accidental discovery at the research center. They're always trying to find a way to manipulate our genes to allow us to drink synthetic blood. That's the whole point of the DeVere Center."

"Why, thank you for that generous thought," Adam cracked. "Synthetic blood means no more human blood, right?"

"Right. So apparently they were working with vampire DNA and human DNA together and they were building some sort of hybrid blood, but in the course of doing that they discovered the location of the human gene that causes the transformation sickness."

"The what what?" Adam asked.

"There's a specific gene?" Jason asked.

"Yes. And knowing where the gene is means they can develop a test to find out in advance whether a human has the proper genetic makeup to become a vampire with no ill effects. This e-mail is a request for funding to develop that test."

"And?" Jason demanded.

"'This is of course not the breakthrough we were hoping for, but it is an interesting and potentially useful side effect nonetheless,'" Sienna read. "'The test would match human mtDNA against—'"

"Why did you stop?" Adam asked. "It was just getting good."

"I heard a car." Sienna sounded far away, and Jason figured she'd walked away from the phone. "Damn! My parents just pulled into the driveway. I have to go."

"No! This is important," Jason cried.

"Print out that e-mail," Adam said.

"And we need the answer to it. Did they get funding? Does the test exist?" Jason added. "Sienna?"

"I'm looking," she answered, her voice tense. "Here it is. My father deleted his reply too. I'm opening it now. . . ."

"You should print a copy. We might need to reference it," Adam instructed her.

"Yeah, and Dad might empty the recycle bin and delete everything before I can get another look at this," Sienna agreed. "Okay. It's going to the printer. If my father catches me doing this, he'll freak."

"Is it printing?" Jason demanded.

"Crap! They're inside," Sienna whispered.

"But did it print?" Adam asked.

"Not yet."

"Sienna—" Jason began.

But the line went dead.

SIXTEEN

Jason stared at the cell phone as if he could will it to bring back Sienna.

Adam reached over, picked up the phone, and hit end. "I'll get her back," he said, starting to redial.

"No!" Jason snatched the phone away from him. "If she's hiding in her father's study and the phone rings, it could give her away. We don't want her to get caught."

"Right. Sorry. Let's just hope she hasn't been caught already," Adam said darkly.

"I don't think there's anything we can do now except wait to hear from her." Jason ran his hand through his hair, frustrated. He hated not knowing whether Sienna had managed to get away with it or not.

"Out with it," Adam said.

"Huh?"

"Why do you care so much about the transformer whoosie-whatsit?"

"Transformation sickness."

"Yeah, that. Are you planning something I should know about? Like, oh, transforming into a vampire?" Adam demanded.

"My aunt Bianca caught me with Sienna the other

day," Jason explained. "She gave me a choice: Become a vampire, or she tells Sienna's parents about us."

"And Sienna gets sent away," Adam said thoughtfully. "Got it. But you're not actually considering transforming, are you?"

"Wouldn't you?"

Adam thought about it. "Would I want to become a vampire and have looks, money, power, and long life? Seems like a no-brainer."

"But?" Jason prompted.

"But if I were a vampire, then I wouldn't be . . . human," Adam said. "I'm not sure that's a good thing. Plus, there's the having to drink blood issue."

"You see my problem," Jason said, shaking his head. "I keep going over and over it in my mind, but I can't decide."

"And then there's some kind of sickness?" Adam asked.

"Transformation sickness is what happens to some humans when they transform into vampires," Jason explained. "Basically there are three possibilities: You're totally fine, you die instantly, or you slowly go insane."

Adam whistled. "Seems like pretty bad odds. Two of those possibilities bite. Hard. No pun intended."

"That's probably why their scientists suggested developing a test for it. The vampires aren't thrilled when one of them dies or goes crazy, either."

"So that's what the test is about," Adam said thoughtfully. "If you could find out in advance that you would be okay—not, you know, dead or crazy—at least you'd know what you were getting into."

"Exactly," Jason agreed.

"Then your course of action is clear," Adam declared. "If that test exists, you have to take it!"

The next morning, Jason got to school so early that he was the first car into the parking lot. He'd left Dani to fend for herself—he was so eager to find out if Sienna was okay that he didn't have the patience to wait for his sister.

Adam pulled in on his Vespa half a minute later. "Is she here yet?" he asked.

"Nope." Jason peered at the line of cars waiting to get into the school. He shaded his eyes against the sunshine. "There she is!" he cried, relieved. Sienna's Spider was almost hidden between Van Dyke's huge Hummer and Erin Henry's Escalade. Jason's heartbeat slowed, and he relaxed a little. He'd been afraid he would show up at school only to find out that Sienna had already been packed off to France.

He and Adam jogged over to her as she parked. "What happened?" Jason called.

Sienna rolled her eyes. "I felt like Sydney on *Alias*," she joked. "Doing computer espionage . . ."

"Lookin' hot," Adam joked along, leering. Sienna gave him a light—vampire light—shove, and he almost fell over.

"Anyway, I got what we needed. It finished printing about two seconds before my father walked through the door," Sienna told them.

"Well?" Jason asked.

"He funded the research," Sienna said. "They were supposed to have a prototype of the test ready by Christmas."

"So it will definitely be ready by now," Adam said. "What are we going to do about it?"

"We?" Sienna asked.

"Yeah. I'm in." Adam frowned. "What, you think I'm only good for the go-between mushy romance stuff?"

"I want to take the test," Jason told Sienna. "I want to know if I can become a vampire."

"Even if you can, that doesn't mean you should," Sienna said quietly.

"But at least I'll have all the facts."

Sienna nodded. "So what do we do?"

"We need recon," Adam said. "Can you get into the lab?"

"Sure," Sienna said. "I'll just say I'm there to visit my father."

"But you can't go when he's there," Jason pointed out. "Otherwise he'll find out what you're doing."

"So I'll wait for a day when I know he's *not* going in to the center," Sienna agreed.

"Cool. Then you just have to sweet talk one of the scientists into showing you the new test," Adam said. "They'll probably be psyched to demonstrate it, anyway, and then you'll know how it works."

"And we can do it on me," Jason said.

Sienna smiled. "It's a plan!"

When Jason got home that afternoon, Dani was already in the kitchen eating Häagen-Dazs straight from the carton.

"Hey," he greeted her. "I haven't seen you all day. Did you catch a ride home with Ryan?"

"No." Dani's lower lip began to tremble, and she swatted at a tear in her eye.

"Are you crying?" he asked, concerned.

"No," she said again. She stuck a spoonful of Dulce de Leche in her mouth.

"Yes you are," Jason told her. "Is it Ryan?"

"No."

"Can you say anything but no?" Jason teased gently.

She dropped the ice-cream carton onto the counter and turned to face him. "It's not Ryan, it's his parents. They suck."

Ah, the vampire parents make their appearance, Jason thought. *I knew it was only a matter of time.* "They told

Ryan he couldn't date a non-vampire," he said aloud.

"Yeah," Dani sniffled. "It's so unfair! I'm not going to spill their secret."

"I know. But they don't like human-vampire relationships," Jason told her.

Dani narrowed her eyes at him. "Wait a minute," she said. "Is that why you and Sienna——" Her cell rang, singing out the theme from *Grey's Anatomy*. Dani grabbed it and hit talk. "Ryan? Oh hey, Belle. It's true. He told me at lunch today."

She covered the phone with her hand and glanced at Jason. "Can you put the ice cream away for me?"

He nodded. *Belle has an even bigger project to keep her mind off Dom, now,* he thought, as his sister headed out to the pool, detailing her conversation with Ryan. *A broken-hearted Dani.*

Jason grabbed the ice cream and stuck it back in the freezer. He knew it was hypocritical of him, but he was relieved that Dani and Ryan had had to break up. Sure, he was thinking of becoming a vampire himself, but somehow he still didn't like to think of Dani getting involved with one.

Thank God Bianca never talked to Dani about the possibility of transforming, he thought. He knew his sister was impulsive enough to do it without thinking it through, if it meant she could stay with Ryan.

Jason headed upstairs, feeling like a jerk. He wasn't

sure why he had such a double standard for Danielle dating a vampire. *Once we figure out how to do the test, I'll talk to Dani about the transformation situation,* he thought. *I just need to get all the information first.*

By the time Friday came, Jason was exhausted. The weeks he'd had to sit out of swim practice while the crossbow wound had healed had taken it out of him, and he'd been training hard lately, trying to get back to optimum speed. But he knew that wasn't why he was so tired. It was the waiting that was getting to him. Waiting for Sienna to find time to get to the DeVere Center. Waiting to find a few stolen moments with her when they could actually talk. Waiting to find out if he could become a vampire, if he could change his life forever without dying or going insane.

He came home from school and dropped facedown onto his bed. "Thank God it's the weekend," he muttered to himself. He was definitely sleeping late tomorrow.

The phone rang. When Jason picked it up, he was shocked to hear Sienna's voice on the other end of the line. "What are you doing?" he cried. "You said we couldn't use the phone!"

"I couldn't help it, I just had to talk to you," she said in a rush. "I'm on a pay phone, so I think it will be okay."

"All right, but hurry," Jason said nervously.

"I went to the lab, it was no problem," Sienna said.

"The guy showed me the whole thing, how to do the test and everything. It's really simple. It tests DNA, so we need a strand of your hair or a mouth swab or something."

"Okay," Jason said. "That's easy enough."

"Yeah, but here's the thing," Sienna said. "We need the equipment at the lab to do the test. We need to physically be there."

Jason thought fast. "They're closed for the weekend now, right? Is everybody out of the building?"

"Everybody leaves by eight or eight thirty," Sienna replied. "Why?"

"We'll go at eleven. That should give us enough of a buffer—all the workers will be gone by then."

"Eleven o'clock tonight?" Sienna sounded surprised.

"Sienna, if I have to wait for one more day to take this test, I'm going to explode," Jason said.

"Okay," Sienna began.

"And besides," Jason rushed on. "It's my life we're talking about. It's my future. I have to know what the possibilities are. Otherwise I'm just thinking about it over and over with no way to make a decision. It's driving me crazy."

"Then we'll do it tonight," she agreed. "But Jason, you know there are guards, right? There's a whole security system."

"I know," Jason said. "We'll just have to break in!"

SEVENTEEN

Jason grabbed his keys from the dresser, jogged downstairs, and headed out the door. He had to see Adam. His friend's father was the sheriff, which meant that Adam had read practically every police report ever filed. Who better to plan a break-in with?

When he got outside, Jason saw Bianca just getting out of her car. "Hi, Aunt Bianca," he called, pulling open the door of the Bug.

"Jason, wait." Bianca strode over to him. "You haven't given me an answer yet. Are you going to undergo the transformation?"

"I'm still thinking," he said truthfully.

"What's to think about?" Bianca replied quickly. "You know what you would gain: power, prestige!"

"I don't care about that," Jason told her.

Bianca gave a wry smile. "I forget how young you are. Of course you don't care about that now. But you will. Trust me," she replied. "I'm your aunt. I just want what's best for you. I want you to have health and long life. That's something your mother would want for you too. Anyone who loves you would."

She put her hand on his arm. "Accept the gift. There's no end to the wonderful things you can have if you become one of us."

Jason looked at her hand. The nails were bitten to the quick, and her red nail polish was chipped. He pulled away, startled. Aunt Bianca was all about appearances. Her nails were always perfectly manicured.

"Aunt Bee . . . are you okay?" he asked. "You seem really stressed out lately."

"I have a lot of things on my mind," she replied. "A lot of people to deal with."

Jason frowned. Was she saying there were bad people to deal with? Or bad vampires? Jason had no real sense of just how many vampire communities there were in the world like DeVere Heights. Were there turf wars? Political differences? Had Bianca become involved in some sort of vampire struggle she couldn't handle?

That's unlikely, Jason thought. *She's too powerful.* "Listen, I'm still thinking about transforming. I really am," he assured her. "But I have to go now."

Bianca stared at him, her eyes suddenly cold. She pulled her hand away. "Don't think for too long!" she snapped. "I'm not going to keep your secret about Sienna forever."

"I won't. Just . . . just keep this between us for a little longer," he said. "Please."

"Maybe I should talk to Danielle," Bianca said, her eyes narrowing. "She might be more willing to make a change than you are."

"No!" Jason cried. "Just give me another day or two. I promise I'll give you an answer then."

"Fine," Aunt Bianca sighed, and suddenly she threw her arms around him and hugged him tightly. "You know how much I love you, don't you? You and Dani both."

"Of course," Jason said, surprised at her sudden warmth. "We love you, too."

Bianca released him and turned away abruptly. "See you later," she called, walking into the house.

Jason climbed into his Bug. He wasn't sure he'd ever get used to Aunt Bianca's sudden mood changes, but he was very relieved that he'd managed to convince her not to tell Dani about the transformation. Or at least he hoped he had. The way Bianca was acting lately, he was a little worried she might just change her mind and tell Dani all about it anyway.

"Dani," he murmured thoughtfully. He was going to the lab tonight. He'd find out for sure whether he could become a vampire or not. Why not find out for his sister at the same time?

Jason jumped out of the car and ran back inside. Dani was still out by the pool, on her cell. But her bag sat on the table in the hall where she always left it. He grabbed it and began rummaging around inside.

"What on earth are you doing?" Bianca asked, peering at him from the kitchen table.

"Oh. I, uh, forgot to get this DVD from Dani. She said I could lend it to Adam." Jason turned so that his body blocked the bag, then he pulled out Dani's hairbrush and stuck it in the inside pocket of his jacket. "Bye, Aunt Bee!" he called. Then he was out the door.

"Let me get this right. You want me to help you break into a top-secret vampire laboratory monitored by security guards and a high-tech alarm system so that you can use outrageously expensive scientific equipment to test your own DNA," Adam said an hour later.

"Is that a problem?" Jason asked.

"No, not at all," Adam replied with a grin. He jumped up and grabbed a backpack from his closet. "Just wanted to be sure I had it straight. So, let's see . . . we'll need a couple of lock-picks, probably a smoke bomb or two, in case we get caught. . . ." He rummaged around in the messy closet, pulling things from boxes and shelves. "Flashlights for all of us, walkie-talkies. Ooh, a taser! We better bring that—"

"Are you insane?" Jason began to laugh. "We're not infiltrating the CIA."

"But we could, my friend, as long as we had the proper tools."

"Where did you get all this stuff?" Jason asked.

"Shh. If I told you that, I'd have to kill you."

"From your dad's office, huh?" Jason guessed.

"I never reveal my sources," Adam said, stuffing his equipment into the backpack. "How about a dog whistle? There are probably German shepherds. In the movies, whenever you break in somewhere, there are German shepherds. Or Dobermans. Do you think they'll have Dobermans?"

"I told Sienna we'd meet her at eleven," Jason said. "I'll drive."

"Okay." Adam followed him toward the door. "Maybe they'll have pit bulls instead. Pit bulls are trendy. . . ."

When they got to the DeVere Center, Sienna's Spider was already parked along the street outside the ivy-covered wall of the property. Jason pulled up behind her and cut the engine. He got out of the Bug as Sienna climbed out of her Spider.

"Hey there," Sienna called softly.

"Hi. I brought Adam along to help." Jason gestured to his friend, who was wrangling the overstuffed backpack out of the car.

"I didn't bring anything to deal with the gates," Adam called. "Should I go back and get some dynamite?"

"Just ignore him," Jason told her. "He's a little overexcited."

"But look at those gates," Adam said. "They're huge!"

Jason glanced up at the wrought iron gates. They stood at least twelve feet tall and had sharp spikes on the top. "How *are* we going to get through those?"

"Relax, spy boys," Sienna said. "We don't need the nitro and detonators tonight. I borrowed Dad's key card. The gates are no problem." She led the way over to the edge of the stone wall that surrounded the center. "We have to stay out of sight of the gates until the security guy goes by. Then I'll open them."

"How did you get the key card without your dad noticing?" Jason asked in a whisper.

"Same way I always used to 'borrow' his credit cards without him noticing," Sienna said with a wink. "I'm crafty."

"How often does the security dude go by?" Adam asked, slipping into a camouflage jacket.

"Every ten minutes. I've been watching him," Sienna replied. "We have to stay far away—he's got a dog with him."

"I told you!" Adam said, nudging Jason.

"*Shh!* Here he comes," Sienna said. They all fell silent as the guard slowly walked to the gates, his boots crunching on the gravel of the driveway. He came straight up to the gates and peered through the iron bars onto the street.

Did we park far enough away? Jason wondered, suddenly paranoid. Their cars were to the side of the gates, so he hoped the guard couldn't see them from where he stood. His dog gave a soft whine, and he said something to it. Then they heard him crunch away again. None of them spoke for a minute or two.

"I think he's far enough away now," Sienna whispered. "Let's go." She pulled the key card from the pocket of her jeans and held it up to the electronic pad mounted on the stone wall. Her eyes met Jason's. "Ready?"

He nodded. "Let's do it."

Sienna swiped the card through the slot. The gates gave a loud *clang* and began to swing outward.

"That was loud," Adam whispered.

"It only seemed loud to us," Jason assured him, hoping he was right.

Sienna led the way past the gates as soon as they had opened wide enough to squeeze through. On the other side was another electronic pad, and she swiped the card again. The gates halted, then began to swing closed. "No reason to let them open all the way," she whispered. "Someone might notice that."

Jason nodded. "Where do we go now?"

Sienna pointed across a wide lawn. A two-story building loomed on the other side. Jason couldn't tell how big the place was; all the windows were dark, and there was no real light but the moon.

"There's a door near those bottlebrush trees. You see it?" Sienna asked.

Jason squinted into the darkness. He thought he could make out a faint blue light near the black blobs of the trees.

"Is that a light over it?" Adam asked. "A safety light or something?"

Sienna nodded. "Yes. It's the closest entrance. We need to get in before the security guy comes around again."

"Come on," Jason said. He took off running for the blue light, moving as quietly as he could. The others followed. As he got closer, Jason could see that the blue light was just a dim bulb next to a plain door. No windows, no signs—just a door with a tiny night-light illuminating the keypad next to it.

"This is a back door," Sienna said breathlessly. She swiped her key card. "It has double security. I need to enter a code, as well."

"Do you know the code?" Jason asked.

"I memorized it. My father keeps the codes written on his calendar. They change every week."

"It's been seven and a half minutes since the security guy passed," Adam said, jogging up to them. "Hurry!"

Sienna punched five numbers into the keypad. Nothing happened.

"When do they change the codes?" Jason asked. "Is it before the weekends?"

"I don't know," Sienna replied, biting her lip.

"I hear the guard," Adam whispered frantically.

"Try again," Jason told Sienna.

She took a deep breath and slowly punched in the numbers again. There was a soft *click* as the door unlocked. Jason yanked it open and ushered his friends inside. He pulled it closed again just as the security guard came into view on the lawn outside. They all held their breath, waiting to see if he had spotted them.

"I don't think he saw us," Jason whispered after a minute.

"I put the wrong number in the first time," Sienna murmured. "I hit the three instead of the six."

"It doesn't matter now, we're in." Jason squeezed her arm. "Nice job."

She smiled at him, her expression playful now that the danger had passed. "Thanks. Let's get to the lab. We've got to do this quickly and quietly and just hope none of the security guys hear us."

Inside the building, the hallways were lit with faint green lights every ten feet. Once Jason's eyes had adjusted, he found it pretty easy to see where they were going. The part of the building they were in looked just like the science wing at DeVere High: lots of rooms filled with lab tables and standard equipment like microscopes and test tubes. But Sienna led the way past all that, and into another wing.

This area was different. The lighting was the same, but here there was a faint humming sound that pulsed through the air. Jason thought he could actually feel it like a vibration in his body. "What is that?" he asked.

"Machinery," Adam answered, keeping his voice quiet. "I had to get an MRI once when I hurt my wrist, and the room it was in felt like this—all magnetized."

"He's right," Sienna said. "There's a lot of high-tech stuff down here. All the testing equipment. MRIs, CT scans, PET scans, X-rays . . . plus a few things I don't even know the names of. We have some toys that other labs don't have."

They reached the end of the hallway and went down a flight of stairs. "We're below ground now," Sienna whispered. "They keep the most sensitive machinery down here because it stays cooler. And here's the test room we're looking for." She pushed open a heavy door and stepped inside. Jason and Adam followed.

Once the door had closed behind them, it was pitch black. "I got this!" Adam said. Jason heard him fumbling around, then a flashlight beam cut through the darkness. "Bet you're glad I brought these," he said, handing a flashlight to Jason and another to Sienna.

"I am," Jason agreed. "I don't think we can risk turning on the lights."

"No, but we do have to turn on all the equipment," Sienna said. She began punching power buttons, and various sleek black machines sprang to life with low beeping noises.

Jason examined them, baffled. "I've never seen anything like this before," he said, peering at a two-foot-square box. It had a single opening on the top that looked like a shallow bowl. "Is it a centrifuge?"

"Kind of," Sienna replied.

"Then what's this?" Adam asked. He was staring at a tall, thin machine with a slot in the side. "Am I supposed to stick a dollar bill in here?"

Sienna laughed. "We're going to stick a DNA sample in there. I don't think a dollar bill will help much!"

Adam shook his head, impressed. "This is truly beyond. I mean, I've been in the police CSI lab, and let me tell you, the Malibu police have serious money compared to most cops. But they have nothing like this stuff."

"I'm not sure *anyone* has stuff like this," Jason said slowly. "Regular research labs . . . do they know about this technology?"

"Not all of it, no," Sienna admitted. "The whole point of this center is to work on vampire research. We've had a lot of time to develop new technology, and we . . . uh . . . have pretty good funding. It's a very high-tech place."

"High-tech? It's astronomical-tech!" Adam exclaimed. "I don't even know what these machines are."

"Honestly? Neither do I," Sienna told him. "But the lab technician was more than happy to show me how they work. He explained all the science, but I was too nervous to pay much attention. I doubt I would've understood most of it, anyway. I remember which buttons to push and that's about it."

"How did you get him to talk so much?" Jason asked.

"Well, first I told him who my father was. And then I flirted with him," Sienna said matter-of-factly.

Jason raised an eyebrow.

"I smiled at him and acted impressed," Sienna clarified. "The guy spends half his life in an underground lab with a bunch of computers. It doesn't take much to make him talk. I think he was just psyched to speak to someone other than himself."

"I know just how he feels," Adam cracked.

"Let's get on with this," Jason said. "Before we get caught."

"Okay. I have everything turned on, and I'm telling the main computer to set up the human genetic test for one subject." She typed a command into a keyboard set up beneath a flat screen monitor on the wall.

"Make it two subjects," Jason corrected her. "I

brought some of my sister's hair. I figure we may as well test her, too. Aunt Bianca will want her to undergo the transformation at some point."

"Okay, let's see . . . here it is, multiple subjects," Sienna said, clicking on a box onscreen. "We're set. We need to get the samples on slides and put them in the slot."

"I am the slide master," Adam announced, rummaging in one of the cabinets. He pulled out a box of glass slides and began to lay them out on the counter. "Slides, I understand. This DNA-reader-thingie I do *not* understand. Does it have a name?"

"Not that I know of," Sienna said.

"Then I hereby christen it the DNAbilizer," Adam announced. "Jason. Hair."

Jason reached up to pull a strand of his hair out.

"Wait!" Adam said. "Make sure you get some skin on the end of it. The DNA is in the skin, not the hair."

Jason obediently pinched his scalp and yanked out some hair. Adam slipped on a plastic glove, took the hair, and began preparing a slide.

Jason reached into his pocket and pulled out Dani's brush. "Can you hold the light for me?" he asked Sienna. She aimed her flashlight at the brush while Jason pulled out a few strands of hair. He studied the ends. "I can't see well enough to tell if there's any skin on the ends," he said.

Sienna leaned in close to him and examined the hair. "Neither can I," she finally said. "Let's make slides for a couple of pieces of hair. Hopefully the DNAbilizer will be able to find DNA to read on one of them."

Jason chose a few strands and handed them to Adam, who put each hair on its own slide.

Then Sienna took the slides and fed them into the slot in the DNAbilizer. Each slide disappeared soundlessly into the machine. Then a series of knocking sounds began, growing faster, then slower, and then starting the entire process again.

"What's it doing?" Adam asked.

"Performing the test," Sienna said. The knocking cycle stopped, the machine now whirring softly.

"All in that one machine? We don't have to do anything else?" Jason asked.

"The DNAbilizer is actually about five machines in one, based on what the technician told me," Sienna said. "They like to streamline everything here."

"Well, what's taking so long?" Adam demanded.

Sienna gaped at him. "It's isolating a single strand of DNA for detailed analysis. How fast do you think that can happen?"

He shrugged. "It would probably take a week to get DNA results at the CSI lab. So I'm thinking it should take about three seconds here."

"We have advanced technology, not a magic wand," Sienna said. "It takes a while."

"Shh!" Jason hissed. "I hear something."

They fell silent. From out in the hallway came the unmistakable sound of footsteps.

"Turn off the flashlights," Sienna whispered frantically. They all shut off their lights. The computer monitor glowed in the darkness, casting an eerie bluish light over all the black machines.

The door opened.

Wordlessly, Jason grabbed Sienna's arm and pulled her back into the shadows behind the DNAbilizer. Adam crouched below the counter he'd prepared the slides on.

A security guard stepped into the room, propping the door open with his foot. Some of the green light from the hallway leaked into the darkness. The eerie glow backlit the guard, making him much easier to see—Jason hoped—than he, Sienna, and Adam were in the shadows.

Jason felt Sienna's hand grasp his, her fingers cold. He looked at her, and she gestured with her head toward the monitor. Data had begun scrolling quickly down the screen, numbers changing faster than the eye could follow.

In the doorway, the guard frowned. He reached for the light switches. Jason's breath caught in his throat: If the lights went on, they'd be discovered for sure!

EIGHTEEN

Beeeeep!

The DNAbilizer let out a loud final sound and turned itself off. On the monitor, the numbers vanished and a message flashed up: DIAGNOSTIC COMPLETE.

In the doorway, the guard chuckled to himself. "Damn machines!" he muttered, stepping back outside. The door swung shut behind him, and the room returned to darkness. Jason held still, his heart slamming against his ribs. Sienna waited beside him, not moving.

Across the room, Adam slowly crumpled to the floor. "Oh, thank God," he whispered. "I totally froze in the wrong position and got a leg cramp!"

Jason bit back a laugh. He could see Sienna and Adam also struggling not to crack up. The relief of not getting caught was making them all giddy.

"That was close," Sienna said finally. "It's a good thing the DNAbilizer is fast." She clicked on her flashlight and crossed over to the keyboard. She typed in a command: display results. The monitor went blank. A green light clicked on over the slot in the machine, and one of the slides slid back out. Jason took it. It was his hair, short and blond.

On screen, a report appeared: S∪ʙⱼᴇᴄᴛ #ɪ. COMPATIBLE.

A tingly feeling shot up Jason's spine. He locked eyes with Sienna. *Compatible.* He could do it. He could become a vampire if he wanted to. He could be with Sienna. Forever.

The green light went on again, and another slide popped out.

Adam grabbed it. "Uh-oh," he said.

Jason pulled his gaze away from Sienna. "What?"

"Subject number two, incompatible," Adam said, gesturing at the monitor, where Jason could read the words for himself.

"Oh, no," Sienna murmured. "Dani . . ."

The green light came on again, and a third slide shot out. The monitor added a new line: S∪ʙⱼᴇᴄᴛ #₃. INCOMPATIBLE.

"Wait. What?" Jason said. "What does it mean, subject number three?"

"We did two slides from the hair on the brush, remember?" Sienna reminded him. "It probably thinks each slide was for a separate person. Here, I can make it give more detailed info. We can check." She typed in another command: Display details. Immediately a long list of numbers appeared under the heading S∪ʙⱼᴇᴄᴛ #ɪ.

"See? That's everything about you," Sienna told him. "The mtDNA markers are displayed in red."

"Maybe I should print it out for future reference," he murmured.

"Now here's Dani," she said, as the monitor displayed the detailed results for subject number two. "And here's the mysterious subject number three. It will all be the same data. . . ." Sienna's voice trailed off. The numbers appearing underneath subject number three were *not* the same. They could all see that. The numbers displayed in red were different numbers. Not all of them, but enough to prove that this was not the same person.

"That's not Dani," Jason said slowly. "And it's not me. The numbers are different."

"Maybe somebody else's hair was in Dani's brush," Sienna suggested. "Kristy's?"

Jason grabbed the hairbrush and began pulling out individual strands. Some were only seven or eight inches long, some were more than a foot long, and all were dark.

"Is there a way to tell if the subjects are related to one another?" Jason asked Sienna. His stomach was cramping. He had an idea who subject number three was, but he really, really wanted to be wrong.

"I think the number of shared DNA markers indicates that," Adam told him.

Sienna toggled back and forth between the results. "Well, all three subjects have a lot of markers in common," she pointed out.

"I'm pretty sure that means all three subjects are related," Adam said.

Now Jason knew exactly who those hairs belonged to. He knew exactly who the incompatible subject number three was. He ran his hand through his hair in agitation.

"Jason?" Sienna asked. "What is it?"

"Subject number three," he whispered. "It's not Kristy. It's my Aunt Bianca."

NINETEEN

"But it can't be!" Sienna exclaimed.

Suddenly a whole lot of things were starting to make sense to Jason. "I'm pretty sure it can, actually," Jason replied. "She's been acting totally weird. She plucked out all her eyebrows the other day."

"Dang," Adam muttered.

"That doesn't mean—" Sienna began.

"It's not just that," Jason interrupted. "It's the way she's acting. You saw a little bit of it in the pool house, Sienna. Aunt Bianca has a different personality every thirty seconds."

Sienna shook her head in disbelief. "I don't want to believe it, but she certainly was acting weird that day."

"Bianca's been acting crazy, but it never occurred to me that she really *was* crazy," Jason said, his head spinning. Aunt Bianca was incompatible with the vampires, but now she *was* a vampire. And she was going mad. She had the transformation sickness.

"Jason." Adam's voice cut through his thoughts. "We have to get out of here."

"You're right." Jason tried to shake off his worry.

"I'll figure out how to deal with this once we're safely away from the lab."

Adam pulled the remaining slides from the machine and shoved them in his overstuffed backpack. Sienna typed "Delete Diagnostic" into the keyboard, then turned off all the machinery.

Adam shut off his flashlight, pulled open the door, and led the way out.

"There's a closer exit," Sienna whispered. "It's that way." She pushed Jason in front of her and brought up the rear. Jason appreciated her concern—he knew he wasn't thinking too clearly at the moment. What was going to happen to Aunt Bianca? How was he going to break the news to her?

"Crap!" Adam muttered. He held up his hand, signaling for them to stop. "Look."

Jason glanced up—and froze. A camera was mounted in the ceiling, its red light focused like a laser as it swept slowly across the hallway. "Two more seconds and it'll be right on us," Jason said. He turned to Adam. "Take off your jacket."

Adam whipped it off and tossed it to Jason. "Get close together," Jason ordered. Then he flung the camouflage jacket over their heads.

"Now run!" Adam cried. Huddled together, they raced for the nearest door. Adam elbowed it open, and they all hurried inside.

"Damn! I was so busy thinking about the key codes, I completely forgot about the cameras," Sienna cried. "Did they see us?"

"I think Jason got my coat over us in time to block our faces," Adam replied. "But they definitely saw a bunch of idiots running around under a camouflage jacket."

"My father will murder me if I get caught breaking into the center with a couple of humans," Sienna said. "This is so far beyond what's acceptable to the Council."

"Are you kidding?" Adam cried. "My father will murder me if I get caught breaking into anything, anywhere, with anyone. He's a cop! He's the *sheriff*! His son is not, repeat *not*, allowed to commit crimes."

"Everybody calm down," Jason ordered them. "The longer we stay near that camera, the faster they'll find us." He took off down the hall and pushed open the first door he came to, holding it open until Sienna and Adam got inside.

Jason scanned the room. It was another lab, this one without any super-secret vampire machinery. There were windows in the far wall. "Quick. Out the window!"

In one fluid motion, Sienna moved across the room and unlocked the window, sliding it open and peering outside. "Okay, I know where we are," she said, as the two guys joined her. "But the gates are way on the other side of the building. We'll have to climb the wall and then walk back to the cars once we're outside."

"The wall is covered in ivy," Adam said. "It shouldn't be too hard to climb. Unless, you know, there are dogs nipping at our heels—although that might be quite the motivator. How do we know where the guards are?"

"I think we just have to chance it," Jason said. "They must've seen us on the camera. They'll be looking in the building first."

"Then let's go." Sienna climbed out the window and took off toward the wall.

"No fair," Adam muttered. "She has super-human speed."

"So let's not hang around," Jason said. He swung his legs through the window, jumped down, and sprinted after Sienna. He heard Adam running behind him.

By the time Jason reached the wall, Sienna was halfway up, climbing the vines like a rope. He grabbed on to one of the leafy branches and pulled himself off the ground. Any second he expected to hear the barking of dogs. Or to see a spotlight go on and catch him, like in a prison-escape movie.

But suddenly he was at the top of the wall. He straddled it, then reached down a hand and hauled Adam up beside him. "I don't see anyone following us," Jason said.

"That's no reason to stay here talking," Adam replied. He swung his legs over and climbed down the other side. Jason followed more slowly.

Sienna was waiting at the bottom, her expression serious.

"What's wrong?" Jason asked.

"I turned my cell back on and there was a message from Belle," she said. "It's bad."

Jason's throat went dry. Had the security guards called Sienna's father already? Were they caught after all?

"It's about Dani," Sienna went on.

"Dani?" Jason repeated, surprised. "What about her?"

"She took off with Ryan," Sienna said. "She told Belle they were going to Le Fleur."

"The hotel?" Adam asked, frowning.

"What hotel?" Jason demanded.

"It's mostly for honeymooners. It's a very private inn on the beach," Sienna said. "That's the thing. Belle is worried. She thinks Dani and Ryan are so upset about having to break up that they might have gone there to do something drastic."

"Drastic like turning Dani into a vampire?" Jason asked.

Sienna nodded.

"But they can't!" Adam cried. "The test showed that Dani is genetically incompatible with the vampire genes. If she undergoes the transformation, she could go insane. She could die!"

"All true," Jason said grimly, already running for his car. "But Dani doesn't know that, does she?"

TWENTY

Jason headed for his car at a dead run. He had to get to Dani. If he was too late, if she'd already undergone the transformation. . . .

He couldn't even think about it.

When they got back to where the cars were, Jason didn't hesitate. He jumped into the Bug and started it up. Adam squeezed himself into the tiny backseat, and Sienna took shotgun. "Where is this hotel?" Jason demanded.

"It's just up the coast a few miles," Sienna said. "Ryan's family owns it. That must be why they went there."

Jason hit the gas and screeched out onto the road, heading for Pacific Coast Highway. As he drove, he fished his cell out of the glove compartment where he'd left it when they broke in to the lab. He hit speed dial for Dani's number.

"We're sorry," said an electronic voice. "The wireless customer you have reached is unavailable or has traveled out of range—"

"Dammit," Jason muttered. He hung up and dialed again.

The same message greeted him.

"Her phone's not working," he told his friends.

"If she's really planning to do this, she probably doesn't want to be reached," Adam pointed out.

Jason slammed his fist against the steering wheel. "I knew she would do this if she found out about transforming! She doesn't think before she does things."

"You never told her?" Sienna asked. "About your aunt wanting the two of you to become vampires?"

"No. I wanted to get all the information first," Jason said. "I wanted to prevent Danielle from doing something like this. I didn't want her to even know it was possible to turn into a vampire."

"Well, if you didn't tell her, who did?" Adam asked.

"Ryan must have," Jason said. "If he's done it, if he's turned her, I'll kill him."

"Slow down," Sienna said, putting her hand on his arm. "There's no way Ryan would do this on his own. He would never in a million years try to talk Dani into transforming. None of us would. We all know how dangerous it is." She paused, then went on carefully. "Do you think it could have been Bianca's idea?"

"She told me she wouldn't say anything to Dani," Jason said, not wanting to believe that his aunt would do such a thing. "She promised."

"But she's not herself, Jason," Sienna said gently.

"Bianca has the transformation sickness. We know that now. There's no telling what she might do."

Jason whipped the Bug down the ramp onto PCH. He floored it, picking up speed. How long had Dani been gone? How long did it even take to complete the transformation? Was he too late already?

Frantic, he grabbed his cell and dialed again. The same message answered him. He hung up and dialed Aunt Bianca's number. The phone rang, and then her voice mail picked up. "Aunt Bianca!" Jason yelled into the phone. "I need to talk to you! Dani's in danger. If she transforms, she'll get sick. You have to help me stop her." He hung up. PCH was only two lanes here, with sheer bluffs on one side and a steep drop down to the beach on the other.

"There!" Sienna pointed to a sign. "That's our exit. Go slow, the road isn't paved."

Jason hit the brakes as he made the turn onto a dark, narrow lane. He wouldn't have even noticed it was there if Sienna hadn't told him. The Bug skidded on the loose gravel as they went downhill toward the Pacific.

"Here." Jason shoved his cell at Adam. "Keep trying Dani." Adam turned on the speaker and hit redial, but Dani's phone didn't pick up.

"Doesn't matter. We're here," Sienna said.

Jason turned the Bug into a small parking lot near

a white Cape Cod–style inn with an antique gas lamp glowing outside the front door. He shut off the engine, grabbed his cell phone, and leaped out of the car, running for the entrance. The lobby was tiny— just a wooden desk and a big fireplace with a couple of overstuffed chairs in front of it.

The woman at the desk jumped when she saw Jason racing in. "Can I help you?" she asked, frowning.

"Ryan Patrick. Is he here?" Jason demanded.

"We need to see him. It's urgent," Sienna explained.

The receptionist checked her computer. "Yes, he has cabin six," she said. "I'll call over for you."

"Never mind," Jason said. He was already out the door.

"I saw a sign for the cabins this way," Adam told him. "Down the stairs."

Jason veered to the right and hurried down the steps that led toward the beach. Several private cabins lay spread throughout the dunes, each with a cabin number lit by a tiny lantern. He spotted cabin six right away.

"Dani!" Jason yelled, racing toward the cabin. "Dani!" He pounded on the door, but there was no answer. Jason tried the knob. The door swung open, unlocked. The cabin was empty.

A wave of panic washed over him. Where was his sister? What had happened to her?

"We'll search the whole place," Sienna said, sensing

his terror. "Don't worry. We'll find them. We'll stop them."

"I'll check the bar," Adam called, sprinting back up the steps.

"I'll check the hot tub," Sienna said, disappearing in the other direction.

Jason wasn't sure where to check. While he thought about it, he pulled out his cell and hit redial.

The phone rang, and then Dani's voice answered. "Jason," she hissed. "What is going on? You've called me about twenty times. This better be an emergency!"

"Oh, thank God," he cried. "Are you okay? Where are you?"

"Jason—"

"I'm already at the hotel. Now tell me exactly where you are," he said sternly.

"On the beach. Down by the water," Danielle answered, confusion in her voice now. "What are you—"

"Stay there. Don't do a thing," Jason instructed. He hung up and rushed to the stairs that led from the dunes down to the sea. As he reached them, he almost crashed into Adam, who was on his way back from the bar.

"She's down on the beach," Jason told him. "Go get Sienna."

Jason kept running, down through the dunes and onto the flat stretch of beach. He dreaded what he might find there. What if Dani had already transformed?

Four tall tiki torches had been set up on the sand near the sea, with a thick blanket spread between them. Jason could see Dani and Ryan sitting there, a bottle of Champagne in a bucket and a picnic dinner laid out in front of them.

Dani scrambled to her feet when she saw him. "Jason," she cried angrily. "I can't believe—"

"Have you done the transformation yet?" he demanded.

Both Dani and Ryan just stared at him.

"Have you?"

"No," Dani said, a tinge of worry creeping into her voice. "We're just having dinner."

"Look, Jason . . . ," Ryan began, just as Sienna and Adam raced up.

Danielle gaped at the new arrivals. "What on earth—"

Jason took his sister's arm and drew her to one side while Sienna and Adam went to talk to Ryan.

"Let go," Dani said, shaking him off. "I can't believe you—barging in on my date! What's wrong with you?"

"You're not supposed to be with Ryan," Jason said.

"You're not supposed to be with Sienna," she pointed out.

"Okay, point taken," Jason agreed, running his hand through his hair. "You're okay?"

"Yes." Dani's voice softened. "Why?"

"Dani, you can't become a vampire," he said. "Not ever."

"Aunt Bianca said I could," she replied. "She told me—"

"I know what she said, but she's wrong," Jason interrupted. "She didn't tell you about the risks, did she? She didn't tell you about transformation sickness."

"No," Dani said slowly, suddenly seeming very small and unsure.

Jason took her hand and pulled her down onto the sand, then sat down next to her. "Aunt Bianca isn't really . . . she's not herself lately," he said. "She has something the vampires call transformation sickness. It's what happens to some humans who turn into vampires. The thing is, some humans can't handle the change, and they die."

Danielle gasped.

"Others don't die, but they get sick," Jason continued. "Mentally, I mean. They go insane. There's a test for it, and I took the test tonight. I took a sample of your DNA, and I tested that as well. It said you were incompatible, Dani. Your body couldn't handle the transformation."

Dani pulled back, tears in her eyes. "You're lying," she said. "Aunt Bianca turned into a vampire years ago. Nothing happened to her. She's not sick." But Jason could tell that Dani was already doubtful.

"Think about it, Dani. Think of how weird she's been acting lately," he pressed. "And when Tyler was in town, he stole something from the Lafrenières. Now, I'm not saying it was right. Far from it. But Aunt Bianca wanted to have him killed because of it!"

Danielle covered her mouth in horror. "I can't believe it," she murmured. "Poor Aunt Bee." Dani stared down at her toes, buried in the cool sand. "And that's what would happen to me?" she asked at last.

"Yes. I'm sorry," Jason said simply.

"Thank you, Jason," she whispered. "Thank you for finding me. We were planning to . . . later. We figured since we had Bianca's blessing, it would be okay. Ryan's parents couldn't be mad with Bianca on our side."

"Ryan!" a voice cut through the air. "Where are you?"

Jason jerked his head toward the sound. A tall, broad-shouldered man was striding down the beach toward them, his brown eyes blazing. He had blond hair cut military short, but Jason suspected that if it was a little longer it would be curly—like Ryan's. The man had to be Ryan's father. He stalked across the sand, practically mowing down a couple taking a romantic moonlit walk. They stopped in their tracks, took in the group by the blanket, and turned back toward the cabins.

"Dad? What are you doing here?" Ryan asked.

Yep. The man was a lot more guard dog than puppy dog, but Jason had been right.

"I got a call from the manager. She saw you checking in with a girl, a human, and thought I should know about it!" Mr. Patrick snapped. "I knew it would be Dani." His eyes swept over Jason's sister, and Jason moved closer to her, protectively.

"You were planning to transform her, weren't you?" Mr. Patrick continued. "Because your mother and I forbade you to see her."

"It didn't happen," Jason put in quickly.

"Yeah, Dad, we didn't do anything," Ryan added.

"Who are you?" Mr. Patrick demanded, ignoring his son and staring at Jason.

"I'm Dani's brother. I . . . we . . ." He gestured to Sienna and Adam. "We found out what was going on in time to stop them."

"The important thing is that nothing happened, Mr. Patrick," Sienna said coolly.

He nodded.

"And right now, there's something even more important that you need to know," Sienna went on. "Something about Bianca." She quickly filled him in.

Mr. Patrick sighed and shook his head. "I'll inform the Council. They'll need to hear about this right away," he said. "Come on, Ryan." He turned and marched away without a backward glance, clearly expecting Ryan to follow—which Ryan did, with an apologetic look over his shoulder at Dani.

"Why don't we all get out of here?" Adam asked. "I feel we may be spoiling the vibe for the actual honeymooners."

"I just want to be home," Dani answered miserably.

Jason pulled her into a quick hug. "You'll be there in a few minutes," he promised. Sienna wrapped her arm around Dani's shoulders, and they all walked toward the car.

"She only told me how great it would be," Dani said, her voice so soft, it was almost as if she were talking to herself. "She kept saying it would be her legacy to me. That I'd live a really long time, and that I'd be totally rich because I'd inherit everything from her, and that everyone would be okay with Ryan and me being together."

"Bianca's ill, Dani," Sienna reminded her. "I know she wasn't trying to hurt you."

Jason looked at Sienna across the top of Dani's head. "Speaking of Bianca," he said grimly, "we have to find a way to help her—before she goes completely insane."

TWENTY-ONE

"Okay, showtime," Jason said as he pulled the Bug into his driveway after dropping Adam off at his house. "Are you ready to go in there and show our parents what happy, normal, non-acquainted-with-vampire teens we are?"

Dani nodded, her eyes glassy with shock.

"Hey, Dani . . ." Jason hesitated, not knowing exactly what to say. "It'll be all right. You're all right. You had a close call tonight, but you're okay."

She nodded again, then forced a smile. "Thanks for riding to my rescue."

"Yeah, you looked real happy to see me when I showed up," Jason teased gently.

His sister smiled again. A little more convincingly this time. "Look at me. I'm a happy normal teen! And I don't believe in vampires!" she exclaimed. "How was that?"

"Oscar-worthy," Jason told her.

Dani opened the car door. "Let's do it."

Jason followed her up to the house, and they walked inside together. They found their parents in the living room. The TV was on, but neither of them was watching it. Mr. Freeman sat on the couch, frowning, and Mrs. Freeman paced up and down the length of the room.

"Hey, we're home," Jason told them. "What's up?" Because something definitely was.

"Did either of you talk to your Aunt Bianca tonight, by any chance?" Mr. Freeman asked.

"Nuh-uh," Jason answered for both of them. He'd *tried* to talk to Bianca, but she hadn't answered her cell.

"She just packed up and left," Mrs. Freeman burst out. "No note, no good-bye, nothing! I just don't understand what's going on with her."

Could she be feeling guilty about what almost happened to Dani tonight? Jason wondered. But when he thought about it, it seemed more likely that his aunt's disappearance was just another sign of her mental deterioration.

"She'll probably call you in a few days to say she's jetted off to Italy to buy shoes or something," Mr. Freeman said reassuringly.

"Yeah, that sounds like Aunt Bianca," Dani agreed, her voice shaking just the tiniest bit. Enough that Jason knew she was thinking about what was happening to Bianca's mind. And what had almost happened to Dani herself.

But then Dani sat down next to her mother and

took her hand. "Really. Don't worry, Mom," she said, her voice strong now. "Aunt Bianca will be fine. I know it."

And Jason believed her.

She's okay, he thought, relieved. *We got to her in time. Dani is truly okay.*

"How's Dani doing?" Sienna asked the next day at lunch with Belle and Adam.

"She's still a little shaken up," Jason admitted.

"Poor baby," Belle said sympathetically.

"She's going to be fine, though. Dani always has a fast recovery time. She's a bounce-backer," Jason added.

"I found out from my parents that Ryan's dad called an emergency session of the Council last night," Sienna informed them. "I thought my parents would freak when they heard about us breaking into the center. But instead the whole Council is thanking their lucky stars that we figured out what would happen if Ryan transformed Dani. If she underwent the transformation and got sick, it would've been a huge tragedy. They're all thrilled that we prevented it." She smiled at Jason. "We actually sort of ended up looking like heroes."

"I *am* extremely heroic," Adam commented. "It's the chin. I have a strong chin, the chin of a hero." He put his hands on his hips, mock-superhero style. "Do not fear. My chin and I will always be here to protect you. We are available for any mission. And we will fearlessly continue to search the web for news of vampire hunters and other dangers to our special friends." He winked at Sienna and Belle.

"I feel very safe now," Jason told Adam, as Belle and Sienna laughed. "What'd the Council say about my aunt?" he asked Sienna.

"That the center is trying to find a cure for transformation sickness," Sienna explained. "Until they do, the Council will keep tabs on Bianca—if she ever shows up again. They've got people out looking for her, but it seems as if she's just vanished. I hope she's all right."

"I hope so too," Jason thought, his mother's worried face flashing into his mind. "I wonder if she knew she was getting sick. Maybe that's why she was so worried about her 'legacy.' It might explain why she was in such a rush to get Dani and me to transform."

"I think she must have known deep down, on a subconscious level," Sienna answered. "The mood swings she got from the transformation sickness definitely upped her intensity too."

"I hope we'll hear from her again soon," Jason said. "Nobody can help her while we don't know where she is." He, Sienna, Belle, and Adam considered this in silence for a long moment.

"My parents gave me some other interesting news," Sienna said, finally, an unexpected smile tugging at her lips.

"Well, lay it on us," Adam demanded.

Sienna leaned across the table, took Jason's face in her hands, looked him in the eye for a long moment, then kissed him. And kissed him, and kissed him, and kissed him.

"Woo-hoo!" Jason heard Adam whoop.

"So is the news that it's okay with your parents if you're with Jason? Or is it something else?" Belle asked, deadpan.

Sienna grinned, breaking the kiss. "They said that as long as I promise faithfully not to transform Jason, they give us their permission to get back together. And the Council is cool with that too."

"I wasn't expecting that," Jason said. "Not that I'm complaining."

"Like I said, we ended up looking like heroes for the way we handled the Dani and Ryan sitch. That's a big reason my parents and the Council are willing for us to be together. You've given them a big reason to trust you—*another* big reason, that is. Also . . ." Sienna hesitated.

"Also?" Jason prompted.

"I think that everybody's a little afraid that if they don't give us permission to be together, I'll just transform you right now whether they approve or not. They know that we know it's safe for you," Sienna explained.

"*C'est bon!*" Adam exclaimed. "And . . . I'm out of French."

"I'm so happy for you guys," Belle told them.

"Me too," Sienna said, her eyes on Jason. "And if we're still together, say, after college, then my parents agreed they'd feel differently about you becoming one of us—if that's what you want—since we know for sure that the transformation sickness won't affect you."

"We'll still be together," Jason promised her. "I know it."

Jason bounded into the house after swim practice on Wednesday. Life was good. He had Sienna. He'd just beaten his best time in the medley. And, oh yeah . . . he had Sienna!

"You look happy," his mom commented.

"I am. How about you?" he asked, realizing that his mother actually looked happier than she had lately.

"I'm a lot better now that I've heard from your aunt. Bianca called this afternoon from the office. All la-di-da, like I had no reason to have been worried. She'd just had to fly back to New York to see a hot new up-and-comer in a play." Mrs. Freeman shook her head. "I figured my little sister would have got a bit more mature by now, but I guess not. I'm just relieved that she's okay."

"Me too," Jason said. And he hoped she stayed okay for a long time.

"What do you say we make some of Dani's favorite jam thumbprint cookies?" his mom asked. "She seems blue-ish to me these past few days. I expect it's boy trouble—not that she talks to me, I'm only her mother."

"Sure. Why not?" Jason answered. He hadn't helped his mother make cookies since he was a little kid. But it could be fun. And his mom was right: Dani definitely did seem like she needed cheering up. She hadn't said anything to him about what was going on with her and Ryan, but he had the feeling she was having a hard time.

"Great. Go wash your hands and we'll get started," Mrs. Freeman said.

"Why do I have to wash my hands?" Jason mock-whined. "I was just at swim practice. My hands were submerged in water for hours."

She laughed. And Jason was struck by the thought of just how hard it would be if he did let Sienna transform him someday. He'd never be able to tell his mom or his dad the truth. There'd always be this *thing* between them. This huge secret.

Jason headed into the kitchen with his mother. *It isn't even something Dani and I could both do, even though she knows the truth about the vampires,* he thought as he started to wash his hands. His sister had no choice but to remain human. And maybe he should too. It's what he was. It's what his family was.

But now that Sienna knew Jason could safely undergo the transformation, how would she feel if he decided not to? Would she think that meant he didn't love her? Or didn't love her enough to want to be with her for her whole life?

"I think you're probably clean enough," Mrs. Freeman commented, pulling him away from his thoughts. "We're baking, not performing surgery."

Sienna and I will work it out together when it's time, Jason decided as he dried his hands on a paper towel. *We always do.*

"Don't eat the last of the cookies," Dani warned him on Friday night. "Those are mine. They were made for me."

"They were made *by* me," Jason countered. "I should get a couple more."

"Nope. All mine!" Dani told him. She looked down at her skirt. "I don't know if I should go with the Diesel. Maybe I should change. What do you think?"

"When you start talking about clothes—and I assume you are, since you were looking at your skirt when you asked the question—it's like Adam talking about movies. I pretty much have no idea what you're saying," Jason confessed.

Dani ran her hands down her short—way too short, Jason thought—brown skirt. "Just, do you think it looks good?"

Looks good for Ryan? Jason wondered. "Well, it's longer in the back than the front," Jason told her. "Is it supposed to do that?"

"Yes," Dani said, all *duh*. "It's called a fishtail."

"And are those straps doing anything?" There were these two thin strips of webbed material that ran from the waist of the skirt to the hem. They were like luggage straps or something. "Are they supposed to show?"

"I really shouldn't have asked you," Dani commented.

"You really shouldn't have," Jason agreed.

"Maybe I'll go try on my new—" The doorbell interrupted her. "That's for me!" Dani exclaimed.

Jason followed her to the hall. He had to admit that he was a little curious to see if it was Ryan picking her up. Although it was hard to imagine Ryan's dad being okay with that—after the hotel fiasco.

Dani pulled open the door and Jason saw Kristy and Maria standing on the porch. But, more importantly, he also saw Sienna pulling her car into the driveway behind them. Jason smiled. He couldn't help himself. When he saw Sienna, he smiled.

"Love the Diesel," Sienna told Dani as she came in.

"Thank you!" Dani replied. "I was trying to get an opinion from my brother and it was hopeless."

"He's fashion illiterate," Sienna agreed.

"No more mocking of the guy," Jason ordered. "Where are you three off to?"

"We're going to Thai Town," Maria told him. "Dani needs to see Kevin, the Thai Elvis, do his thing. And also, we need coconut rice."

"Have fun," Sienna called as they hurried out.

"We will, don't worry," Kristy called back. "We're going to make sure Miss Dani has lots and lots and lots of fun."

"Why do I have the feeling that they're trying to take Dani's mind off something—like when the guys took me to Venice Beach after our sort-of breakup?" Jason asked as he closed the door behind them.

"Because you're right. I was talking to Belle before I came over, and she told me Dani broke up with Ryan," Sienna answered.

"Weird that I have to figure out what's going on with my sister through the best friend of my girl-friend," Jason told her.

"Belle and Dani have gotten really close. She's been like a big sister to Dani through the Ryan romance. It's been good for Belle, having something to think about other than all the bad stuff. She's starting to get over Dominic's death, I think."

"It's been good for Dani, too. It's not like she could talk to Kristy or my mom about the difficulties of dating a vampire," Jason pointed out. "Did Belle say anything else?"

"Just that Ryan's hurting right now," Sienna told him.

"Dani, too," Jason said.

"She'll recover. They both will," Sienna promised. "In fact, word on the grapevine is that there's a very cute boy who is going head over heels for Dani. A *human* cute boy," Sienna added before Jason could ask.

Jason grinned. "Now that that's settled," he said happily, "what should we do tonight? What are you in the mood for? Anything you want . . ."

"Well, we never got to really dance to our song," Sienna answered. "How about we go back to the yacht and finish what we started? It'll be even better under the stars."

"And that's okay with your father?" Jason asked doubtfully. "The place *is* a floating motel, so I hear."

"He trusts us," Sienna replied. She pulled a key ring out of her pocket. "He gave me the keys himself."

"So should I call Adam and Belle?" Jason teased. "Since we're trying to finish what we started. They were there the first time and all."

Sienna gave an exaggerated frown. "Sadly, Belle and Adam are on their way to the Cinerama Dome. Belle thinks the bar at the theater is the perfect place for Adam to meet some simpatico, movie-loving chicks."

Jason grinned and opened the door for her.

"Should we take my car or yours to the marina?" Sienna asked.

"Yours. Definitely," Jason answered.

"You know the Spider is temperamental," Sienna warned. "We could end up breaking down."

"That's what I'm hoping for," Jason confessed. "Nothing better than breaking down with you and getting stuck somewhere." He leaned close and whispered in her ear. "All alone."

Sienna gave him that slow, sexy smile of hers and grabbed his hand. "My car it is."

An offer you can't refuse ...
A new series by Todd Strasser

Kate Blessing is a smart, normal high school junior—whose family members just happen to be mobsters. The crimes they commit are small: designer knockoffs, DVD bootlegging. Kate's family may be unusual, but they're *family*. She loves them. Besides, without them she wouldn't have her indoor pool, three-hundred-dollar jeans, and Caribbean vacations.

But when Kate's mom moves out, the family business is suddenly up for grabs. Someone has to step up. Dad may be the face of the mob, but it's not long before the princess is running the show. . . .

MOB Princess

These families mean business.

MOB Princess
For Money and Love
TODD STRASSER